Forgiveness
The Anthology of Elijah Jefferson

by Quain Holtey

Table of Contents

Title Page

Copyright Page

Table of Contents

Author's Note

Bound

Heresy

Creation

Shock

Aftermath

Chronological Order

Beginnings

Solitude

Purpose

Lost

Broken

Forgiveness

About the Author

Author's Note

It's hard to believe that I wrote Forgiveness four years ago. Since then I've written...a lot more, though at the time of writing, Forgiveness: The Anthology of Elijah Jefferson remains my only published work (outside of a few short stories I published before then).

While I'm working on some new, exciting, and much longer things now, those are sadly going to have to wait, as it's my goal to get them traditionally published. Still, I felt like there was something else I could do for Forgiveness. A last hoo-rah, as the children say, and I've always wanted a hardback copy of it on my shelf.

Inside you won't find any changes, really. Some spelling errors were fixed that I noticed after the initial release, and my author bio is updated.

In the first paperback edition of Forgiveness, I wrote out the chronological order of each of the stories, but that always felt like an awful work around. I know some people, some of my family and friends included, want to experience the narrative chronologically, but putting the onus on the reader to constantly flip through the book to find the correct story numbers, then flip back to the chronological list, makes for an absolutely awful reading experience.

That being said, I don't want to ignore the written order, either. I love the different sense of tension it brings to the narrative, and it calls back to how I originally wrote this story; an out of order mess of flash fiction following a month's worth of word prompts.

So, instead, I've decided to put both orders in this book! I'm making the change to all formats; paperback, ebook, and, for the first time, hardcover. Ideally, this will let you choose how you'd like to experience Elijah and Shadow's story, whether it's your first time through, or a reread (while also filling out the 100 page requirement for the name to appear on the book's spine (did you know the first edition was 86 pages? I was 14 pages away from being able to tell where my book is on my shelf, and I'm still kinda salty about it.)).

Whether this is a reread, or you're experiencing this story for the first time, I want to extend my heartfelt gratitude. Forgiveness holds a special place in my heart as my first published work, and I hope that, by the end, these characters and this story hold a special place in your heart as well. Thank you.

With a Smile,

Quain Holtey

Bound

1

Hot lemon, parsley, and smoke whisk me from my half-asleep. The crackling of the nearby fire breaks through the trees. I breathe in deep through my nose, and as the cold air floods my body, the unmistakable smell of cooked fish laid under the medley of citrus and herbs feeds my lungs. I clutch my stomach as it pinches and groans. How many days have passed since we last ate? My body rises in answer to my question. A need to get closer.

Too fast. My head swims, and my vision crowds with black static. I'm not sure if I'm still standing. The sudden blast of nausea sends me spiraling into the infinite, but eventually I find some semblance of myself, and I swim back into consciousness. The static recedes to my periphery, but doesn't fully retreat, and the blood drains from my ears, giving way to the sounds of laughter now piercing the deep night, marrying itself with the crackling fire. I peek through the bushes into the warmth.

Burt tin foil packages bursting with food sit still steaming and splayed on the lap of a man. He seasons each package before handing one to his wife and one to his young son. My stomach stabs as drool drizzles uncontrolled down my chin. Maybe, if we're lucky, they'll slip to sleep soon and leave their lemon rinds and bones for us. Maybe more if the young boy doesn't like fish...

The laughter stops. It was so sudden, I look away from the young boy's tin foil package to see the mother clutched close to her husband, both staring at the bushes. No, at me. Directly at me. I look down and witness myself standing stark in the clearing, my dirt-covered body bathed in the yellow-red firelight.

The smell of food had been too tempting. I had stepped out from the bushes. My heart entered my throat, and I turned to run, but the black static's revenge was well-timed. The darkness that I had held at bay flooded my vision once again, plunging me into the void. My head grew too heavy, and I felt the dull thud of my body as it hit the ground.

"Hey!" a man's voice said, though it was muffled through the blood in my ears. He no doubt held a stick at the ready, prepared to protect his family from the mud-caked, unclean, malnourished animal that stumbled from the forest onto their perfect family camping trip. He had no care that I was trying to flee myself, that I didn't want to be seen any more than they wanted to see me. If you just give me a moment to get right, we'll leave you in the peace you desire. I'll be back for the bones.

"Here, let me help," he said. His voice cradled my head, and his arms wrapped easily around me, tugging me skyward. When had he come all the way over here? What was he doing?

"Christ, you weigh nothing," he said. "Can you stand?"

I didn't answer. Color finally peaked through my vision.

"Can you talk?" he asked. He carried me towards the fire. Its warmth helped drive away the cold with every inch, and its light cast our silhouette in a long, jittering outline.

"What are you doing, Harold?" the woman asked. "Don't bring him over here."

"Look at him, Judith. He can't even speak," he said. "Here." He tossed me about in his arms before setting me on the log next to where he was sitting, his wife half hung off the opposite side. "Take a seat here, you can have my food. I'll make myself one of the extras." He kept one hand on my back and with the other, moved his charred tin foil package onto my lap, a plastic fork stuck vertical, piercing the fish inside.

Without question, I ravaged the package. I ate the cooked halved lemons whole, their sweet-sour citrus exploded in my mouth. The fish was covered in herbs and butter, and the skin gave way to hot white meat inside. Soon, there was nothing but bones left, so I resorted to chewing them, our hunger not yet satisfied.

I dragged my two fingers along the bottom of the foil and shoved them in my mouth. The three strangers stared at me with varied expressions of horror, curiosity, and pity. Amidst the food, I had all but forgotten where I was.

"Here," Harold said, handing me a bottle of water. "You must be thirsty, too."

"... thanks," I said. I stole away the bottle and took a sip. Soon as the water hit my lips, I couldn't help but chug its entire contents. I must have been thirsty, too. Harold offered me another bottle, which I made sure to sip slowly this time. "Thanks," I said again.

"Don't mention it," he said. "What's your name, son?"

An innocent question. No harm in them knowing my name, right? "... Elijah..."

"How old are you, Elijah?"

"... What day is it?"

"The first," Judith said. "October first."

"I'm nine," I said. I had missed my birthday.

"Jesus..." Harold said.

"Where are your mom and dad?" the boy asked. I took a long drink. His brow furrowed, and his hands shook. He hadn't touched his dinner yet, and with any luck, he wouldn't touch it at all—more food for us.

"I don't know," I said. It was the first lie I had told them.

Silence descended over the camp like a blanket, smothering the mouths of the family. Had they seen through me? The fire's intermittent crackling would break the silence, but never the tension.

"How long have you been out here, Eli?" Judith asked. She looked nothing like my mother; she was tall and thick, with straight blonde hair that fell across her back, tucked away behind one ear. Yet there was something about her that reminded me of her. Tears welled in my eyes as I remembered her love, but the dry fire fizzled them before they could fall.

"I don't know," I said. "It's starting to get cold again... so maybe a year? No more than two."

"Judith," Harold said. Without another word, she was next to her husband, leaning into one another. Their soft whispers tickled the edge of my ears, but not enough to know their words.

"Here," said the young boy. He had moved next to me at some point and was extending his tin foil plate to me. "I don't really like fish."

I immediately began to devour the meal; though I knew our appetite would not be even remotely satiated.

"My name's Jimmy. I'm nine, too."

Hello, Jimmy.

"Do you like toys? I brought a whole bunch with me from home! Mom and Dad said I could play with them all night if I wanted, since we're on vacation!"

That's nice, Jimmy.

Jimmy continued talking as I ate. He joined the white noise of my chewing, the campfire popping, and his parents' whispers. I finished eating, chewed bones and all, but we were still starving. Two whole meals and it was as though nothing had changed. Our stomach still churned and tightened, and I knew exactly why. I picked up my water and sipped it carefully. I didn't want to do it. Not again. But, the hunger...

"Elijah," Harold's voice broke through my turmoil, "how would you like to spend the night with us? Tomorrow we can take you back into town and get you cleaned up. After that, we can find your parents. What do you say?"

Judith stood behind her husband, holding his hand. She nodded and smiled in agreement, my mother's love in her eyes...

One night. Our stomach twisted with hunger, churning with renewed fervor at the prospect of another meal. My shadow quivered in time. One night. It would last us through the winter, maybe longer. One night.

Yes... we could eat them all in one night.

"Yes, please," I said.

2

The last breath of fire gives me life.

I twirl and twist upward, weaving effortless through the invisible wind.

A maze creates my infinite form,

my life is my separating unconscious.

The first color I witness is red.

Life blooming forth from lifeless mounds around my birthplace.

A Shadow looms over the death dealer,

my screams are the floating nothing.

The grip of death coils around my tail.

It is not the shadow, nor his prey, but the chill of the air that cools my body.

A death quickens the longer I live,

my death is the cooling smoke.

Life is an abstract second of horror.

3

"Mom, you're not listening," I said. I pinned the phone against my shoulder as my knife parted red and green spears from bell peppers. I had put this off all day, telling myself I would call once I had the patience. Had the courage. My bravery had arrived right before dinner. Maybe I just needed something to take my mind off of her while we talked. "I love him."

"And you think that is enough reason to abandon us?" she asked. Her voice distorted through the receiver. "There is more to marriage than being in love. Your father and I taught you that at least." Her accent grew thick as she raised her voice, and memories of stiff dresses and stinging hands flashed through my mind. I closed my eyes and reached for the next vegetable.

I knew she wouldn't understand. I had told Shane she was sure to come up with a litany of reasons why we shouldn't get married. I was too young, he wasn't educated, and of course...

"–he's a mechanic. He cannot make enough money to support you, let alone a family."

...he didn't make enough.

"I know what kind of man he is," I said. "He's strong, and hardworking. He cares about me, more than he cares about himself. There's no one else in this world he, nor I, would rather be with than each other."

Silence and static filled the receiver. I stopped chopping halfway through the onion. Had I done it? Had that been enough to silence her? To prove I wasn't the reckless child she thought me to be? Was it that easy?

"...Lyla, your father and I do not want this for you." The onion stung my eyes. "We want your children to have a better life than we could give you. If you marry this man, they will not have that. You will not have that."

"As long as I'm with someone that makes me happy, I don't care what life I live," I said. My chopping grew furious. How dare she insult me or my family.

"You will say different when you have children of your own."

"*If* having children," the knife cut deep grooves into the cutting board as it slammed down with my voice, "means my life will become miserable, then I don't want them—JESUS!"

Blood spewed forth from a fresh cut in my finger. No, not a cut. I had sliced clean through. The whole first joint of my finger had stayed on the cutting board.

"Lyla? Lyla you do not mean that. Lyla—"

"Goodbye Mother," I said, and hung up the phone. I found a towel and placed it over my finger, which stained the white fabric red.

The front door opened.

"Lyla, did you call your..." Shane trailed off as he rounded the door. A brief pause, then he rushed to my side. "Jesus. What happened?"

4

Their first meal was a rat. Disgusting. Stringy. Its meat tore and squished between their teeth. He didn't know it was wrong, or what his parents would think if they saw him crouched over the half-eaten corpse, and he didn't care. All he knew was their hunger, and how, for the first time since his birth, it was satiated. At least a little.

Shadow knew, however. He had been Bound to plenty of humans before now, and he knew their reactions to such animosity. Yes, he knew all about humans, especially how good they tasted compared to this rat. Their salty, muscle-ridden bodies, with welcoming bone handles for him to hold as he tore through their flesh. Oh, he knew. But his Bind did not. He was still too young, barely any teeth in him. Of course he didn't know what delicacies waited for them in the form of man. Even the ones that doted on his every move, cooing over their "brand new baby boy." Oh yes, they would be scrumptious, to say the least.

For now, though, this rat would have to do. Shadow could tell he wasn't enjoying himself, probably wasn't a fan of the texture, but the satisfaction of a full stomach was too much. He would not stop. The Bind was full, and he could not live without it now. None of them ever could. Soon it would be more rats, then dogs and cats. Then would be the hard times. Raw meat, but none of it fresh. All processed and packaged, sitting in cold boxes waiting to be cooked and drained of life by the very prey they would soon take, but he would have to endure it. He would still be too young for a full human.

Maybe, if Shadow and his Bind were lucky, they could find a newborn no one would miss. Or another child ready to go missing. That would be the perfect transition, though tricky, especially given how much his parents loved him. Shadow and his Bind would have had a much better chance in a foster home, or even out on the streets, but, no, Shadow was Bound to a human in the worst of circumstances: a place to call home, two parents, and soon he would have school with other impossible to devour children. Disappointing.

The Bind finished his rat, slurping its tail into his mouth, filling their stomach to bursting. It would be a month or two before they needed more, but for now, their appetites were satisfied, if not their palettes. Shadow knew his Bind wished he would never have to eat anything like that again. Some gave into the hunger, others didn't. They would go as long as possible before eventually caving to their desires. This Bind was one of the latter. It would be months before their next meal.

Poor Shadow.

5

Investigating Officers: Police Officer Ryan O'Conley, Police Officer Katie Haughes

Incident No.: 092831-24T-2020

Case Description: Domestic Disturbance report.

This is the official transcription of P.O. Ryan O'Conley and P.O Katie Haughes arriving on the scene in response to a Domestic Disturbance report at 4102 12th Street, APT. 712 New York City, New York 11101

P.O. Ryan O'Conley: God damn...

P.O. Ryan O'Conley coughs and gags.

O'Conley: That's rancid. Dispatch we are outside the door to apartment 712 and there's some awful kind of smell in the hallway. Do you know about this?

Dispatch: Be advised, Officer O'Conley, neighbors called complaining about the smell. D.D. was filed due to the number of complaints.

P.O. Katie Haughes: Isn't an odor complaint more suited for building management than police?

Dispatch: Affirmative, however, neighbors said they have attempted to call the landlord and building maintenance to check in on the room but haven't heard any response.

O'Conley: In this neighborhood? Lines up. Next time give us some warning, Dispatch?

P.O. Ryan O'Conley knocks on Apartment 712's door.

O'Conley: Apartment 712, this is Officer O'Conley, open up.

Haughes: Hello? Apartment 712, can you hear us? We'd like to ask you a few questions about the smell.

O'Conley: I don't feel right about this Katie. This smell...it ain't right. Something's wrong.

P.O. Katie Haughes knocks on Apartment 712's door.

Haughes: Apartment 712, is everything alright in there? Hello?

A door opens.

Apartment 710 Resident: What's all the hollering about?

Haughes: Sorry to disturb you Ma'am, please return to your apartment.

710: Disturb me? You ain't disturbing me any more than that wretched stench. Been getting worse for weeks now, and ain't nobody doing anything about it.

O'Conley: Ma'am, do you know anything about the folks that live here?

710: Sure, the Jeffersons. Shane and Lyla. They've got a little boy, too. Um...oh what's his name?

O'Conley: Have you seen them recently? Any of them?

710: Not since before the smell started. You know, I think they left for vacation or something, and left something out on the counter that's been rotting away since.

O'Conley: Did they ever talk about going on vacation? Did you see them leave?

710: Well, no. Come to think of it, they been living here for eight years, and I don't think that Shane has ever missed a day of work, even when his boy was born. That's a man who knows how to provide for his family if you ask me.

O'Conley: Thank you for your help, ma'am. Please, return to your apartment, we'll get rid of the smell.

710: Good.

A door closes.

O'Conley: Mister and Misses Jefferson, we're coming in. Dispatch, be advised we are forcibly entering Apartment 712 on probable cause of a homicide.

Haughes: What? You heard the woman; they're probably just on vacation.

O'Conley: They don't go on vacation for eight years, then they disappear for weeks without telling anyone, and a rancid smell starts coming from their apartment? It doesn't sit right with me. What if somebody's dead, Haughes? What about that little boy?

Haughes: ...Dispatch, be advised we are forcibly entering Apartment 712 on suspicion of a dead body.

Dispatch: Received.

Wood breaks and a door opens.

P.O. Katie Haughes screams.

P.O. Ryan O'Conley vomits.

6

"I don't like this," the Bind said.

What did it say?

I do not care. As though its desires held any precedent to my own. *I own you. I will always own you. I give you power. Life. Do not think for a moment, young Bind, that you are not under my control, and, if I wished, I could kill you as easily as I have any of our meals.*

"I don't think that's true."

Where was this coming from? When had it grown so bold? *What spark of insanity leads you to believe such nonsense?*

"Well, we don't really get along all that well, and I don't think you would stick around if you didn't have to. You would've killed me by now, or at least run away, if you could."

The little Bind. *Perhaps I enjoy watching you squirm.*

"No, that's not it. You get hungry when I get hungry, and you're not hungry when I'm not hungry, but if you didn't need me, you could just leave me and eat someone and then come back. You wouldn't need to wait for me to be there. In fact, it's almost like you need me to want to eat someone too before you eat them, like, you need me to be okay with it. Which I'm not. I just get so hungry. If you really didn't need me, you would just eat them yourself. And..."

Proverbial God, I hate how children ramble. Still, the little Bind had figured some of it, and at such a young age. It was far from adulthood, we had only been bound for eleven years, yet already it knew more than many Binds ever cared to know. I have no doubt its mind will give me nothing but trouble if left unchecked. Why couldn't it just be normal? Bask in the power I give it and let us eat our fill instead of running its mouth on half discovered truths?

You wish to test me?

That shut the little Bind up quick. If only I could prolong the silence. Maybe I could scare him a bit...

You think I cannot leave? We will see how you do out in these woods all by yourself, Bind.

With that I stretched myself thin, fleeing into the unending darkness of the trees and fallen leaves. The forest always has shadows, even in the day. Of course, I'm not able to separate myself from it. Not completely. It is my Bind after all. But children are easy to fool. If I'm far enough away, he won't know the difference between distance and abandonment. He'll beg for my return soon enough.

I can already hear his teeth chattering.

Heresy

7

I hid beneath the trap door in the kitchen. The straw pierced my body as the dark tendrils of my siblings crawled across the floor above me. They whisked out candles and dampened fires, allowing the night's darkness to creep inside. In retrospect, hiding was useless. If I had known what I do now, I would have bound to the burly, bearded Timothy Upperbuckle, who lay asleep next to his wife only a room away, completely unaware of my encroaching demise.

Instead, I waited in my trap.

They had known of my escapades. It was only a few nights ago when Torlin had first witnessed my disappearance, and my answers to his questions did not satiate his curiosity. Now, he was here, leading the charge on my capture. My death.

I knew I wasn't meant to venture here, but I couldn't stop myself from Folding back, night after night, these last hundred years.

The Overworld had such incredible beauty: a moonrise over the endless patched fields of agriculture, the untainted wilds of what is now called the Americas, the ice capped mountains and endless oceans encouraging ignorance between sects of humans. Ah, humans. All the wonders of the Overworld paled in comparison to its inhabitants. Humans, who varied from infants to old men, homeless to queens, each with their own unique stories and personalities. How important they all feel their lives are. Their tiny, momentary lives amidst the cosmos. Candle lights under the unobstructed sun that waver, flicker, and die before a single day is set. Yet, each life still burned, and, for the briefest of moments, their lingering smoke remained in the memories of those closest to them. Useless. Gorgeous. What I wouldn't give to live a life full of meaning, even if it were for just a moment. What I wouldn't give to be human and live in this world without tainting it with my shadow.

The trap door flew open, and the tendrils of those I called family took me back to the land of the Shades.

8

The train lights flickered, bathing the residents in pure darkness for second's fractions every so often. A man took up several seats in the corner farthest from us. His snores betrayed his comfort, yet were no match for the screeching metal of spinning discs that echoed off the tunnel walls.

A woman had joined us on the last stop, younger than the man by far but perhaps only slightly older than Elijah. Her hair cascaded over top her head in black curls, grouped together by some herculean bond. She was pretty, and Elijah's accelerated heartbeat and sweating palms told me he thought so as well. She had chosen a seat directly between us and the sleeping man, right across from the sliding doors through which she had entered.

Elijah himself looked worse than the man on the other side of the car, though, to be fair, Elijah had not had a chance to look human in such a long time. His unnaturally thin body, a product of my punishment, was covered by the canvas jacket. It contorted in awkward shapes, crumpled by the empty space inside. I found myself thinking of how effective a sail it would make should we encounter a strong enough breeze. His unending restlessness would send a chorus of shifting, crumpling fabric around us. Our stomach growled for a long moment. Louder than the snoring.

Screeching drowns all other noises as the train once again grinds to a halt. The power is diverted to the brakes, and the lights' flickers become deep flashing strobes that worsen Elijah's headache. I relish in the long dark, happy for the opportunity to stretch, if only for a few moments.

The doors open to three loud men who burst into the car. Despite the rows of empty seats, they stand. Directly in front of the woman. They speak above the chorus of snores and screeches. They speak loud about nothing. I hate them. They make us feel crowded.

These men need to leave. They are ruining the peace that we were enjoying. We only have so much of this peace left.

"Shadow," Elijah said. A warning.

I recoil back to his silhouette. In my subconscious I had stretched away from him and toward the standing trio. If this had been before, I would have ignored him, but the last time I did that, he enforced the fast. We did not eat for years.

"...where're you going, sweetheart?" one of the men said. He kicked the shoe of the woman in an effort to get her attention. We know better though; We are predators too.

She did not respond, of course. Her averted gaze and recoiled posture said everything necessary. Good. Starve them of the attention they seek. They will move on.

"Hey," the second man said. "The man asked ya a question! You'd do well to answer it 'fore I make ya."

Forceful. Irreverent. Dangerous. Elijah's blood pumped harder, and the lights flickered in time. I could feel his will stretching out. Using my power to affect reality the way I once could.

"Where I'm going is none of your concern," the girl said.

Idiot. She was doing so well.

"Oh, I beg t' differ," said the second man. "Way I sees it, you's alone tonight, and there ain't nothin' more dangerous than bein' 'lone at night here in the city." She refused to answer now, but it was too late. She added fuel to the fire with her few words. It was not her fault. None of this was. It was simply the way we disgusting predators worked.

He laughed. "We'll jus' have t' follow you home then. Make sure you's safe."

Elijah stood and took steps toward the men. I was not sure if he was aware of what he was doing, or if, like me, his subconscious urged him forward. It did not matter. I would not stop his advance like he had mine.

"Stop it," Elijah said. His voice was that of a timid mouse.

"Leave us 'lone, lad," one said.

"Yeah, let the grown-ups talk," said another.

The woman gave a look toward Elijah. Her eyes pleaded for help, but her face contorted in confusion. She could see we wanted to help, and she wanted it too, but what could Elijah do? A poor, lanky boy with a too large coat one strong breath away from sailing across the water. Oh, but she did not know.

Did not know about me.

Elijah's blood coursed through his veins with increased fervor. The lights flickered to match his heartbeat. Thump-thump. Flick-flick. His hold on me loosened, and the pain in our stomach resounded through our bodies.

"I'll tell you again," he said. His voice now filled with my power. "Leave her be."

"Who are you to tell us what to do? Sounds like you need to be taught a lesson in manners, boy." The three men walked towards us. Good. I doubt Elijah heard what they had said with all the blood in his ears, but their advancement was a universal language.

"Shadow," Elijah said. An invitation.

The lights flickered in reverse now, plunging the train car into darkness with only quick flashes of light. The men approached, and I freed myself, stretching to the size of the car, pressing against walls and windows. They saw me in the strobe, and fear engulfed their faces, but it was too late.

I struck faster than the first could scream. With one gulp, only the waist down remained, and slumped to the floor. Dark maroon scattered across the floor before I bent down to finish my meal. The second man stood, frozen in fear. I did not need to be quick with him. I opened my mouth wide and inhaled him in one bite. He was spicier than the first. Delicious.

The last managed to run to the far end of the train and cower in the corner next to the sleeping man. I pulled Elijah closer, dragging his feet across the slick metal. The last man's screams were drowned by the sound of the subway's screeching breaks. The old man slept.

He did warn you, I said, licking back my saliva. I swallowed him whole like the last one, no need for too much blood, but I savored him, crushing his bones between my teeth. He popped like a fish egg.

We pulled into the next stop as I sulked back to Elijah, our stomach now full to bursting. He filled out his canvas coat nicely, he even seemed a bit plump. The lights returned to their normal cadence.

"What... what the hell was that?" the woman asked us.

Elijah did not answer, and we joined the cool night air as the train doors opened.

Speak, Inebriate. May your words be sufficient to shift the mountains and change the Penumbra.

The Father of Shades stood tall on his perch, flanked on either side by my brothers and sisters whose dark shapes attempted contexture with the atmosphere. Our world was nothing like the Overworld where the humans have color and life. Here was nothing but hues of shadow. It was ugly. Unfair. A testament to the fools that called it home and refused to explore.

Why should we have to suffer in a world of drear when we can frolic in life with the humans, who pointedly ignore us? Could they even see us? Did it matter?

Why should we refrain from our desires? I asked. *Here there is nothing, an endless void for us to wither away in. Why experience no joy nor life, when there is no point in our suffering other than self-mutilation? We can indulge. Spread our shapes across the green and blue of the Overworld with no one to stop us. Live with humans rather than hide ourselves away to die.*

Abomination, one of my sisters muttered. Whispers of affirmation spread throughout the formless room. *The Maw should have its way with him.*

If it is an abomination to want more than this dementia, then I accept your praise, I said.

Tell me, Arystic, said Father, *are you aware what your meddling hath wrought? How humanity's beauty, the motivation behind your 'transcendence,' has dwindled into violence and destruction?*

You cannot blame me for their dark ages.

We can and we will! A voice grated to the Father's left. Torlin. *With your free reign, knowledge scatters for sake of conquest devoted to some fictitious higher being! Progress halted. No, reversed. So that you could fill your appetite and run amok throughout the Overworld, spreading war, disenlightenment, and disease in your wake!*

The Father recalled the synod to order: their dissensions of disgust and agreement echoed over top one another in the muted hall.

My betrayer brother was not wrong, of course. When I travelled throughout the world as I pleased, the darkness of home spread over humanity like an eclipse. Why that was, I could not say, but I refused to accept it as unnatural.

If we were not meant to spread ourselves over humanity, I said, *then we would not know of them. More than that, we would not be able to Fold freely to their world in the first place.*

The Maw places humanity in our reach to tempt us, said Father. *To give us acumen.*

Acumen? Over what? To choose to live eternities in dread and pain? To force us into misery so that we can, one day, be devoured by the Maw that gives us such divine life? I spat on the floor, my secretions swirling into the sinking void below. *The Maw knows nothing except to feed on our ignorance, and eventually our flesh!*

The uproar that followed my blasphemy was nothing short of entirely satisfying. Father stared through me in disbelief as the council members debated ways to end the suffering of their ears from my voice. Amidst the various, creative ways of ending my immortality, the consensus landed firmly on the only solution whose results were known to be permanent.

Give the Maw a meal, came Torlin's voice over the clamor.

No, said Father. He never broke his gaze from me. *Your heresy does not deserve reward in the belly of the Maw.* The synod awaited in eager silence, hanging off Father's words. I will admit, I was curious to what punishment he thought befit my crime of life and love.

You wish to live in the Overworld?

What was he getting at? *With my every being, yes.*

Then you shall have your desire. You shall be tethered to humanity. Bound. Forced to live shackled to that which you love so much. You will be Cursed to never leave their side.

Father, please, Torlin said. *You cannot reward his lust.*

He will find no such reward. His newly required sustenance will ensure his punishment. Father's smile was cruel as his gaze bore through me. *As the Maw 'knows nothing except to feed on our ignorance and flesh,' so too will Arystic be forced to satiate his appetite... with humanity's flesh.*

No... you can't. Please. But my words fell on deaf ears filled with the excitement of those I once called family.

10

"I feel ridiculous," Elijah said.

You look ridiculous. Shadow said. His throatless chuckle rose from beneath the stiff cotton and shifting suit jacket wrapped around Elijah's body.

"If I look like a fool, then so do you."

"Focus." Victoria's voice muffled into Elijah's earpiece, her short concise voice reminding Elijah how cute her anger made her. "You look great, Eli. I wish you dressed like this more often. Now please, focus."

"Right."

Sorry, Victoria.

Elijah stood up straight and adjusted his single-looped tie one final time. He was glad for the suit coat, as it hid the thin tail tucked into his waistband which poked from beneath his overlapped tie. He handed his invitation to one of the large, well dressed bouncers that flanked the grand entryway. Without a second glance at the invitation, the guard handed him back the paper and waved him in, his focus taken up by the trio of young women gowned in glitter and smokey eyes behind Elijah.

Elijah walked through the grand glass doorway and onto the marble coated floors, their swirls of black and white reminiscent of twisted taffy. Once confident he was out of sight, he pulled to the right, breaking free from the wave of nicely dressed attendees and finding shelter behind one of the stone columns thicker than any tree Elijah had grown up with. He scanned the room's various displays of ancient weapons, wax figures, and art.

"Shadow, eyes?" Elijah asked.

Don't go anywhere.

Elijah placed his hand on the pillar. A long, thin string of ink dripped up one of the grooves. The bright lights all around the main room sent scattered shadows in every direction, giving the shade plenty of room to grow.

Finally, high above the crowd, he could breathe. He bloomed across the ceiling, a flower whose stem was far too thin, and scanned the two floors below him. Humans had become one of two things: food or Binds. However, these new rules Elijah and Victoria lived by had forced him to pay more attention. Now he had to hunt for specific meals, which taught him something he hadn't had in such a long time. Preference.

Young children with red faces and dripping noses were the ones that popped nicely in his mouth. Women tended to have a nice chew, while men came with the most meat per meal. Older humans were crunchy and brittle, better as an appetizer than a main meal. Tonight, he was on the hunt for one such man in a suit with graying hair and pale skin.

Another benefit of working with Victoria had presented itself soon after they had met; they were almost never hungry anymore. Well, they got hungry, but at least they never starved.

"Any luck?" Victoria called through the radio.

Still looking.

"Still looking, baby," Elijah said. "The issue with an old white guy as our mark is that it describes most of the people here tonight."

"I know. I would have given you a scent if I had anything. Kind of difficult when he's untouchable."

"We don't blame you. No one I know could get a scent from Mayor Ellis, especially with the current measures he has undertaken."

Found him. Second floor. Staring at the vomit of color.

"Shadow says he's looking at the Pollock," Elijah said. Shadow funneled back down to rejoin his Bind. He laid flat against the floor and set himself up to mimic Elijah's movements, settling into Elijah's silhouette.

Let us go.

Elijah moved deftly through the crowd, stopping every so often to make a show of looking at the various displays. Nothing sticks out in people's minds more when the Mayor goes missing than someone who came in and went straight towards him. They climbed the slightly curved stairs, sticking to the exposed stone sides rather than opting for the red velvet carpeting draped down the stair's center.

Why do humans delight in such randomness? Shadow asked. They weaved through the various displays ranging in different sizes, from several meter-long canvases to single square foot pedestals holding ancient pottery. *I understand the beauty of color, but it loses its appeal when smashed together without thought.*

"You can see color?" They stopped for a moment to stare at a tattered bit of rune inscribed cloth. "I would think that, with you being mostly monochromatic, you couldn't see color, or maybe just everything in a red hue."

Yes, I can see color, Shadow said. His shortness could not be overstated. *It is one of the reasons I was drawn to your world in the first place.*

"What were the other reasons?" They moved to the Pollock painting, a piece that seemed to span the width of the entire floor. Lights shown directly on the painting, creating methodically placed coned pyramids.

"I see him," Elijah said. "He's reached the end of the painting, but he's about to move to another exhibit. We need to get him alone."

I must come to your aid once again, Bind. Shadow said. He slithered through the footfalls and scattered shadows of crowded humans until he reached the other side of the painting. He coiled around the mayor's leg, slithering ever upward, around his torso, and eventually his arm. The Mayor went to take a drink from his starry glass, and the glass tipped right before it touched his lips. Profanity and chuckles left his lips as champagne soaked his white shirt, and Shadow reversed his slither to rest beneath Elijah's feet once again. *If I were you, I would make my way to the bathroom before his guards seal it off.*

Elijah ducked through the crowd. He made a rather convincing show of needing to use the restroom, Shadow thought. Once through the swinging door, he made his way into one of the empty stalls, closed the door, and perched atop the toilet so he could not be seen from the gap that ran along the floor beneath the metal walls.

Three breaths later, the door swung open yet again. Footsteps pounded along the echoing tiles, then stopped.

"Christ almighty, you'd think I'd learn to control myself," the Mayor said. The sink bubbled for a moment, then flowed water. "You need to be a picture of strength, Edmond. That's what she said. I cannot maintain support if I appear incompetent."

"Shadow," Elijah said, too quiet for the Mayor to hear during his ramblings, "bring the night."

Gladly. Shadow spread like a dark puddle across the cool floor. Thin as a sheet, he covered every crevice and winding groove. He climbed the walls, sealing shut the doorway and small window that opposed each other on either side of the room. The only ways out.

"What in the hell..." Mayor Ellis said, finally taking notice of the darkening room. He turned around to gaze at the nightmare. "What in God's name?"

Shadow made it to the ceiling. He dripped over every light fixture like wet ooze, and they popped beneath his weight. The last fixture created a spotlight above Elijah's stall before it's pop plunged the world into darkness.

The creaking of metal hinges, its normal reverb absorbed by the black.

"Wh-who's there?" the Mayor asked the dark. "Show yourself."

Shadow had coated himself around his Bind like a blanket, so when Elijah opened his eyes only a few feet from the man, Shadow's own eyes stared crimson at the Major, their glow providing the only light source in this small world. They were the eyes of death. Elijah knew it, Shadow knew it, and now so, too, did Mayor Ellis.

"Are you... what is this?"

"Mayor Edmond Ellis," They said, their mouth a villainous crack of sharp teeth and ruby void. "You willingly traded weapons and drugs for money you used to fund your second campaign. Admit to your crimes."

"I-I assure you I have no idea—"

"Confess," They said, their words drowning out the Mayor's blabbering.

"I-I-I did," he stammered. Good. Quick. "Yes, I did, but once I am re-elected, I will rid the streets of New York of crime and drugs and make the city safe once again." His excuse rang with rehearsal. "It's... It's temporary."

"And what of the innocents who are to be killed with these weapons now? What of the families that will be torn apart by the drugs you supplied for them? The children who will grow up without parents? The parents who will have to bury their children?" The room grew darker as they spoke. What started as a silent night now turned into a reverberating void, whose only salvation lay in the red glow of death's eyes and mouth.

"Th-they're... n-necessary..." The Mayor didn't believe his own words.

The eyes recoiled for a moment. They and the crooked mouth grew in size, raising high to the ceiling. Shadow was amassing himself, tearing himself away from Elijah.

"Edmond Ellis," Elijah said, "you are guilty of crimes too abhorrent to repeat. Your right to this life is hereby revoked, as you have so willingly revoked the lives of others."

"W-wait. Please, don't do this... if you kill me, you're no better!"

"True." There was a pause, and for a moment, Mayor Edmond Ellis believed his plea had struck a chord. A glimmer of hope shown in his eyes, and he uncoiled himself, "but I accepted my demons long ago."

Shadow lunged for the man. The Mayor's screams were smothered in his throat. Crunchy, just as Shadow had anticipated, though there was something else. A hint of vanilla, Shadow thought. As he ate, Shadow dripped off the walls and hid himself once again in his Bind's silhouette.

"The Mayor's guards will be waiting outside the door," Elijah said. "Tori, Mayor Ellis is taken care of, but we need a way out."

What about the window?

Elijah looked at the small window. "Not a bad idea." He pushed against it, and it opened along the bottom, its top hinges not making a sound. Hanging halfway out, Elijah realized they dangled twenty feet above the hard asphalt below.

"Hey Shadow," Elijah said, gathering himself, "catch."

Elijah threw himself out of the window.

11

I stood outside their run-down apartment. Peeled paint and cracked wood; thin walls muffled televisions and old ladies playing cards next door. Seven-twelve hung precarious on the door in front of me, my hand hovering inches away from the wood, ready to rasp out a knock.

Did I really want to be here? I knew exactly how this night would go. Lyla would get mad at me for speaking the truth simply because it was not what she wanted to hear. She would kick me out, her husband would protest, and we would ultimately attempt to repeat this adventure in another nine years with another grandchild. Was seeing him even worth this inevitable failure? Seeing the product of my daughter's mistakes flaunted in front of me? I turned on my heel and took one step before the door opened, revealing a smiling man in an unpressed white shirt and single looped tie, with a tattered jacket and jeans to complete his disheveled ensemble.

"Terah, it's so nice to see you," Shane Jefferson said. "Did you just get here?"

So genuine, so pleasant. Though I suppose someone of his standing had no choice in the matter. Cannot make your way up in the illustrious car repair world without licking some boots, I suppose. "Your top button is undone," I said, and stepped past him and inside.

So, this is where my daughter was living. Or rather, surviving. This single bedroom, wall stained, rat infested hell hole. "Are those cockroaches on the wall?"

Shane turned his head toward the wall so fast I heard his neck pop. Hope told me he had *snapped* his neck right then and there, and I awaited in eager anticipation for him to collapse to the ground. Alas, he turned back with a joking smile only a moment later. That disgusting, genuine smile. "I promise, Lyla and I keep a clean home. Can I take your coat?"

"Where?" I asked. The brief flash of confusion that spread across his brow would have made me laugh if not for the circumstances. I shrugged off my coat, grabbed either shoulder to ensure an even vertical fold, then horizontal over my arm. Perfect. I pressed it flat against my body. "I'll keep it with me, thank you."

"Right... well, Lyla is just in the kitchen making dinner. You can join Elijah at the dinner table while you wait."

We walked into the kitchen and dining area; the tiled flooring throughout would have elicited regurgitation had I already eaten. We walked past my daughter who, unprovoked, pointedly ignored my presence. Off to a good start I see. I sat at the head of the table and, after a moment's hesitation, draped my coat along the back of the chair. My coat was already tainted by the very air of this place, no point in keeping it off hard, stain-covered surfaces. I straightened my skirt, why I had decided to dress up for this was beyond me, and looked up to see my grandson.

I nearly fainted.

What sat before me was not a boy, but a ghoul. Skin stretched tight across bones, no meat on him whatsoever. His clothes fell awkwardly around his skeletal frame. He looked like he hadn't eaten in months.

"Gracious Lord in Heaven," I said. "Do you feed the thing?"

He averted his gaze, which somehow made it easier to stomach.

"Yes," Lyla said. Her first word to me in nine years.

"I don't believe you. Look at him! He's practically dust." I tore my eyes away from the malnourished beast. "Yet you seem to be eating well, Shane."

"Mother."

"What? I am just saying Elijah sits not ten feet from your good for nothing husband in this cramped apartment with nothing but God's grace keeping him from death, while Shane has obviously had his fill of food for a good long while. I feel the need to call child protective services on the two of you!"

Lyla slammed the knife she was holding down on the cutting board. Was one of her fingers shorter than the rest?

"You come here after nine years and not twenty seconds into stepping through the door threaten to take our child away from us?"

Just as I thought. She would get upset with me for simply speaking the truth. When will she grow up? "If that is what's best for the poor thing. Look at him!"

"You act like we don't know! He eats every day; we make sure of it. The doctor says there isn't anything wrong with his health and that he's not malnourished. He just doesn't seem to put on weight."

"I am not surprised. With the type of care you are able to afford I am sure your doctor recommends leeches."

"Okay, all right," Shane said. His arms were outstretched as though taming tigers. "That's enough. Terah, our son is not malnourished. He just doesn't put on very much fat. His metabolism will slow down when he gets older and he'll start to look as healthy as he is."

"How dare you." My blood boiled. A mechanic was going to talk to *me* as though *I* was the problem? No. I stood up and went to Elijah. "If you do not see the problem here, then you are the problem. You disgust me. Come on Elijah, we are leaving. I should have done this a long time ago." I pulled the boy from his seat. He was heavier than his frame made him out to be.

"Get the hell away from my son!" said Lyla. She was coming after me with a knife. My own daughter! What had gotten into her? Can't she see I'm just trying to help?

"Lyla," Shane said. "Put the knife down. Terah, put down our son." Reason met with insanity. As if I was going to listen to the man stealing my grandson's food out from under him.

"You have proven you cannot care for him, like I have always said you wouldn't be able to do.

You cannot care for him, cannot care for my daughter, cannot even care for yourself!"

***

Elijah cowered in fear. He didn't want to be in this stranger's arms, but he had no idea how to get out. Everyone was screaming, and he didn't fully understand why, only that it was his fault. It was always his fault.

Bind, came the familiar voice, *I can make them quiet. All this screaming can go away. Would you like that?*

Elijah nodded into the woman's shoulder. All he wanted was for the fighting to stop. For his parents to stop screaming. For the woman to put him down. If he had known what Shadow would do, maybe he could have said something, but none of the arguing made any sense. And he was just so hungry.

Shadow lashed out like quills across the room, piercing the walls, cupboards, ceiling, and people. He flattened and expanded his quills and cut through bone as easy as muscle, dicing their bodies into thick chunks. Blood sprayed everywhere, and its thick syrup dripped off the walls. The boy started to cry at the horror around him.

But the arguing had stopped.

12

The pianist plucked a soft song in the background of the restaurant, serenading the array of celebrating couples seated at cloth-draped tables atop velvet carpet floors. Not a child in sight to upset the atmosphere. Wait staff moved through the tables with an air of effortlessness, like rats through a maze. Except one, who, through all her mimicry, was still bumping hips against corners and trembling platters on her palm. A uniformed man came out from the kitchen as she went in. The collision would have caused quite the clamor, ruining the ambiance for many a customer, if not for the grace of the man's trained reflexes. He had been where she was at one point, and his patience was spread plain across his face as consolations spewed readily from his mouth to match her babbling apologies.

"So," Victoria said. "How long?" Her voice pulled me from my reverie. I looked back at her, body leaning over the table, her long dark hair tickling the white cloth beneath our still-clean platters. She spoke in a hushed voice, as though sharing a secret, and the sweet smell of wine drifted to my nose from her glass.

"Sorry?" I asked.

"How long have you, you know," she glanced over her shoulder. "Have you two been *together*?"

"All my life," I said. "At least since I can remember, so as early as three or so." Curious, I took a sip of her wine. Its sweet flavor of grapes and cranberries turned sour and rank in my mouth. Why would anyone drink this?

"And it's always done what you've said?" she asked.

As if I need permission to fill our stomach, Shadow chimed in. *I am not some wild animal that needs training, Elijah. Make sure she knows that.*

"No," I said. "We haven't always seen eye to eye. Also, he's not a pet. Hell, he's older than me."

"How much older?"

"God if I know. He says he's with his Binds–what he calls the humans he's linked to–till we die, and he says he's lost count of how many he's been with."

"Well how high can he count?"

I gagged on my drink.

Better watch your mouth, little morsel. I know more than you ever could.

"Yes, but," I said, moving the cup back up to my mouth. "How high can you count, Shadow?"

"What was that?" Victoria asked.

I will make us eat everyone in this restaurant if you are not careful, Bind.

"Nothing," I said, chuckling. Shadow and I had grown closer during our fast, but I think this was the first time he made me laugh.

"So," Victoria said. "This whole vigilante thing. It's new?"

"We're not vigilantes, Victoria," I said.

"Tori, please." She slid her hand over mine, and I noticed how low cut her dress was.

"Right, Tori. The other night on the subway was the only time we've done something like that, and it was the last. Those men could have people looking for them. Families, employers, whatever. Shadow and I didn't come back to the city to start eating people."

A waiter came next to our table and set up a small foldable stand to place our meals upon. Victoria and I sat up straight once again, and with agile fingers the man cleared our place holder dishes and replaced them with steaming piles of pasta and sauce. Why did they bother with the temporary clean plates in the first place? Seems like more needless dishes.

I picked up my fork and began dancing it across my meal. Victoria, however, made no such move. I stopped to look at her.

"There's plenty of good in what you did on that subway, you know." Her eyes didn't meet mine. They were distant, gazing through the floor next to my chair. Shadow writhed beneath me, and her eyes squinted for a moment, no doubt seeing the edges of my opaque overcast shifting with his movements. Few people ever noticed, but it wasn't impossible to see. If you knew what you were looking for. "I looked them up. Two of them were charged rapists, and one had been arrested before for domestic violence. His girlfriend? Her face was swollen so badly I don't think she could see when they took her picture. Broken bones, bruises all over her body... If you and..." She trailed off.

"Shadow."

"...hadn't stopped those men—"

"Killed those men," I said.

"—then I don't want to even think about what could have happened to me that night."

How does she know all this?

"How do you know all this?" I asked.

"I have connections. Listen, Elijah," she met my gaze, her eyes were firelit amber. "This city is filled with people like them. God even the Mayor; if you knew the monstrosities he's done to get back in office... I don't know what agreement you and... Shadow... came to, but people like this need to be stopped. And you have the power to stop them."

Silverware against dishes and the low drum of conversation muted the silence that followed what she suggested. A sudden clash from the kitchen erupted from behind the door, followed by a woman's familiar apologies. Whoever she had bumped into was not as understanding as the first waiter. Not one conversation was fazed, however. It had happened in another room, behind closed doors, so it didn't bother them. They simply went on eating, blissful in their ignorance. Shadow sat still, waiting for the response that was clearly my responsibility to give. He would follow whatever path I chose, it seemed.

I twisted my fork in the pasta and pulled it up to my lips as Victoria watched with bated breath. My thoughts turned to my parents. Would they have wanted something like this for their son? Would this new path Tori presented fulfill what I sought before the subway car?

"Where would we even start?" I asked, then wrapped my mouth around my food.

I weave through the equidistant ocean of weathered stones, each uniformed monolith holding secrets of names and dates in various stages of erasure. The ground mounded at regular intervals, lulling me into security with its ebbs. Flowers in variable states of decay were placed underneath the stones' protection every so often. They painted the green grass brilliant shades of pastels wrapped in vibrant paper.

I stopped. I had found them. Three barely marked headstones placed one right after the other. The first two I had expected: Shane Jefferson and Lyla Jefferson, but the third caught me off guard. It was smaller than the other two by half, and smaller than most other gravestones in the ocean. On its weathered, forgotten face, was Elijah Jefferson. Was me.

"They think I'm dead," I said.

Not much of a surprise, considering the mess of parts we left behind, came my Shadow's response.

"The mess you left, not me."

Right. Sorry. He had gotten used to saying that these last few years.

As surreal as it was to gaze upon my own tomb, it wasn't why I had come. I turned my attention to my parents and opened my mouth to speak, but nothing came out. It didn't feel quite right. Something was missing. I stumbled away and scanned the other headstones until I found the secret ingredient to my visit: two suitable bundles of flowers: one blue iris, the other daisies. She had loved daisies, that much I remember. I brought them back and placed them under their new homes, protected under stones that had never held flowers before. Perfect.

"Mom, Dad..." I said, and any semblance of the speech I had prepared beforehand was lost in a sea of salt and water. I couldn't help myself. "I'm so sorry for what happened. Please know I didn't mean it. I was scared. We all were. I didn't know what to do, and Shadow was just trying to help me. I didn't know what would happen. I didn't know. I didn't..."

Sobs overcame my words as I knelt blubbering to cold stone. No apology was enough. I had known nothing would bring them back for a long time. Our stomach growled, and I became instantly aware of how long it had been since we'd last eaten.

"I'm—I'm going back into the city. I'm turning myself into the police."

What?

"All I've been able to think about these last few years has been how to give you justice. How to honor you. But I'm the one responsible for your deaths. I killed you..."

No, Elijah. I killed them. You had nothing to do with it.

"If I'm locked away, if we're locked away, we won't be able to hurt anyone ever again."

Elijah...

"I've made up my mind, Shadow! This is the only way I can see that's right. The only way I don't hurt any more innocent people."

The silence was peaceful. Wind swept through the trees and hummed through the low stones to create a symphony of woodwind tones. My canvas coat crumpled in the wind.

I stood. There was nothing left to say. I weaved back through the headstones and their rhythmic mounds and left the graveyard. Evening turned to night, and the lights of the city supplied their own sun. I made my way through buildings and streets to the nearest subway station.

God I was hungry.

14

Shadow pushed off the ground, launching us above the cruel wrought iron fencing. We landed with a crunch onto the leaf-covered asphalt path.

The naked trees bathed the night in an ominous, monochromatic hue that would have deterred any sane person. A few steps in and I could see our destination. Its flush stone entryway stood as a ward before the cave beyond its threshold plunged into darkness.

"Sybil's cave," I said. "I wonder what she's doing here."

Living out her Poe fantasies, Shadow said. He reached out, emboldened by the endless darkness, and gripped the gate blocking the entrance to the man-made cave.

"What's that supposed to mean?" I asked. Shadow pulled the gate apart, its metal creaking as it bent and eventually snapped, sending once chained links twisting off into the night.

Edgar spent quite some time here. They found a woman's body, so he couldn't resist, really. He was always drawn to the dark and mysterious. He spent months inspired by those events. Even wrote a piece about it. Shadow slithered back to me as he spoke, tucking himself into the folds of my silhouette.

"Wait, Edgar Allen Poe? How do you know that?" I asked.

Shadow breathed a sigh, though I was entirely sure he didn't actually need to breathe.

Merely a dramatic imitation. *Poe was one of my past Binds. Now, can we eat?*

I froze. Not because it was cold, though it was, and it wasn't because this new information shocked me. I froze because I realized that I never asked Shadow about his other Binds. He's been around for what must be hundreds of years, bound to different lives, and I had never once asked. Hell, I had asked him so few questions in general. I hardly knew him. Aside from our shared hunger, I was bound to a stranger.

"Shadow," I said, still unmoving. "Why are you bound to people? You've told me you're with a Bind from birth to death, but you've never said why it's like that in the first place. Are all Shades bound to humans, or are you the only one? And why?"

There was a long pause.

Elijah, he said. *You have never once prodded. These questions take time to answer, so why ask them here, on the precipice of our hunt?*

"That's not an answer."

Another sigh. *Yes, there are other Shades, just as there are other humans. Though I am the only one bound to humanity, as far as I know. And I am bound to humanity as part of my punishment.*

"Punished for what?"

For loving what I should not. Now, can we please eat?

"I'd like to know more but," I said, and started walking towards the freshly opened gate. "You'll be happier entertaining my questions when our stomach is full." I pressed my finger to my ear. "Victoria?"

"Here," she said. Her voice was muffled through the radio static.

"We're going inside. You're sure she's here?"

"Absolutely. Reports say she uses Sybil's as a kind of hideout."

"All right, we'll probably lose you in the cave."

"Be safe."

"I love you."

"I love you, too."

I moved my arms wide and bent my knees. Shadow's arms engulfed my own, giving me dark, brutish arms tipped with jagged claws. He felt like a cool blanket.

We stepped into the cave; whose damp halls echoed with each of our footfalls. Vapor from the freshwater spring inside condensed along the ceiling, which had lengthened the stalactites during their continual slow drip back to the water below. The round cave was supported by thick pillars, crowding the already small cave and sending any noise shooting back throughout the room. One of these sounds was sporadic and would have been entirely silent if not for the walls' reverb. The sound of breathing.

"Lilliana Crow?" I asked. My question repeated endlessly in the echoes.

The breathing stopped. I walked around the pillar and could hear her footfalls mirror mine on the other side.

Elijah, where is that light coming from?

What was he talking about? It was pitch black.

"Lilliana Crow, you've caused the disappearance of seventeen people over the last six years. You've stolen their belongings, cleaned up your messes, and have always remained outside the law." The sound had changed as we continued our dance. The ground beneath me shifting under my weight. Looking down, I saw the shifting floor beneath my feet. Mounds of... sand?

Elijah, the light!

Lilliana reversed her dance, stepping in front of me and stopping me in my tracks. I swiped with my claws, but Shadow had retreated, and I swung empty fists too far to reach.

"Whoever you are," she said, placing her hand on my chest, "you can join them."

The world swirled, sucking into itself where our bodies connected. I felt myself fold and contort, slipping into the void, condensing into a single point, like being sucked through a straw.

Then out again. The entire process in reverse, like stretching over infinity. The air on the other side was hot, hostile. It burned my skin within seconds. The sun beat heavy and dry over top of us, and Shadow retreated to the confines of my–

Shadow screams. I have no silhouette for him to retreat into. My own opaque shadow was gone. Shadow's screams stopped as soon as they had started, and for the first time the heft of his form dragging my feet was gone. He was gone.

Sweat poured, and I squinted my eyes in an attempt to see anything other than blinding white. Agonizing, impossible moments where all I could feel was searing heat, my body sinking into the ground, and the absence of a piece of my soul.

Eventually my eyes adjusted to the blistering light, and were met by an ocean of endless dunes.

Creation

15

It was a storm that gave birth to the Maw. An angry typhoon that called lightning and fire to scorch the earth before tsunamis buried it, swallowing it down into the endless ocean.

In the midst of this Chaos, Its form was shaped. Molded by the forces of the heavens and churning ocean. Pure energy condensed into primordial rage large enough to swallow the world. Its body was earth shrouded in black mists, and when it opened its mouth, light screamed forth in a beam that evaporated the clouds, revealing the sun once again.

But the Maw was not the only thing born in this Chaos. Flitting through this new world were beings of shadow and light that trailed across the waters. They explored their new home, living in their respective elements, circling each other endlessly, in tandem with the sun and moon.

The Maw reached into the ocean and pulled the earth back from its depths. Land flourished above the tumultuous ocean, and with it, new life. Humanity. They revealed themselves, crawling out of every cave and crevice, infesting the world like insects.

What happens next is lost to time, but what is known is that the beings of Chaos, these Shades and Glints, were separated from this earth by The Maw: given their own worlds in which to explore and make their own, while humanity was free to inevitably ruin this one. Only, they didn't. Through all their failings, the world of humanity flourished, and the inexhaustible Shades and Glints instead ruined their own worlds.

They pleaded with the Maw to let them back into the human Overworld, to let them explore beauty once again, but It refused. The Maw kept the worlds separate, saying Chaos had wrought its own demise, and that they should live in the prisons they had created, else the Maw would devour them, and they would cease to exist entirely.

And so, they did.

16

The firelight assaulted the barricaded door, sending strings of light through cracks and holes which scattered across the floor. Clamoring steel and screams of death filled the air, but inside they were distant. Muffled. The Oda and Tokugawa armies had defeated us long ago, but their bloodlust motivated their current pursuit of my husband, and those kind enough to help us flee from our home were now being butchered in theirs.

"Help me with this," my husband said. He tugged at the buckles and ropes that held his armor in place. I pulled at the ties and loosened the strands, helping him disrobe. With one hand on the front chest piece and the other gripping the back edge, he stooped over and together we slid the armor off. My hand came away covered in hot crimson. The steel scales of his o'yoroi, the same ones that had ensured his victory so many times before, had crumbled under Oda Nobunaga's three thousand guns. A hailstorm of bullets had pierced and bent the now jagged armor into my husband's skin.

"Masako," he said. "There is a compartment. A hatch that will take you beneath the house. You can use it to get out of here. Remain hidden from the *Oni kuso yaro*." Every few words were emphasized by grunts of effort as he knelt and brandished his tanto, its short blade shimmering in the cracked fire light. Never used, always polished.

"No," I said. "No, I will not leave you. You and I will remain together, no matter the cost. Even if that cost is death,"

My husband nodded and placed his hand on my cheek. He smiled through his tears. "I do not deserve you. In this life, or the next."

The screams had dulled to a hum, barely audible in the back of my mind. I knelt beside

Katsuyori, and we stared at each other before death. His eyes sparkled, wet with his love. A love I knew was reflected in my own. Then, the sickening sound of his rent flesh squishing around the blade of his tanto echoed between us. He pulled the blade, then handed it to me before he collapsed, dead at my feet. My vision grew cloudy and wet.

I sat up straight and held the blood-soaked blade in front of me. I pulled.

Hands of shadow flashed out and wrapped around the blade. Their strength held the blade in place, preventing me from fulfilling my promise.

"You have no say in this," I said.

Masako, please, Arystic said. *Do not do this. We can make it out of here, you and me. I can protect you; you know I can. Please do not leave me too.*

"My husband is dead. My people are dead. The time for protection is long past, Arystic. I want nothing more than to join my beloved Katsuyori. To fulfill my promise. And I will spend every waking moment from this point forward trying to if you stop me here."

You have so much more life to live, Masako.

I relaxed my grip of the blade and placed my hand along his. "My life is over now, sweet Arystic. I choose it to be so. You may keep me from dying for the next eighty years, but nothing you can do will help me live again, for I am already dead." His coiled grip loosened, and he slid back into my silhouette. I took position with the tanto once again.

"One day," I said, tears finding their way to the floor, "I hope you find someone that makes you feel as deeply as I feel for Katsuyori. That you may understand my words. I pray that for you, my dear, sweet, Shadow."

I plunged the blade into my stomach; its piercing sting a pale comparison to the pain I already felt. I pulled to the side, tearing my insides and spilling the floor with blood. Finally, I twisted the blade and pulled upward. My world went black, and the momentary agony subsided with everything else.

My suffering was over.

17

Of course I followed her. She knew where he was. She did something to him in that cave. He vanished. And I needed to know.

Where was my Elijah?

I tailed her for a few days. Honestly, I'm surprised my resolve lasted as long as that. Every fiber of my being wanted nothing more than to choke the life out of her. But tonight, I broke. I waited inside her house for her return. She had stopped going to the cave since that night and started coming back home. There was a thin layer of dust over everything, as if even when she came home, she didn't touch anything. Not just the surfaces, like her sofa or the counters, but even the floor was undisturbed, as though she didn't walk, but hovered. Who was this woman?

The deadbolt on the front door tumbled to the side, and the door opened. I waited as she stepped inside and closed the door, relocking it like I knew she would. Like she had done every night she came home.

"Where is he?" I asked.

She turned around with barely a hint of surprise. Was she expecting me?

"Where's who?" she asked. She's toying with me; I know she is. But her smile didn't match her eyes. It was cocked in confusion. Suddenly I wasn't so sure. No, she was playing dumb. She had to be. She knew where he was.

"Elijah Jefferson. What did you do with him?"

Recognition flooded her face, and her smile broadened. She *was* toying with me.

"Oh, the man and his Shade," she said. She took a few steps toward me, and I drew my gun. I hadn't come unprepared. She froze, head cocked to one side. Almost like... curiosity? "They're gone."

"Gone where? What did you do with them?" I couldn't stop my voice from cracking, nor my vision from blurring. "Where's Eli?"

"It doesn't matter. They're not coming back. No one does."

Lies.

I pulled the trigger. I pulled it again. And again. Each shot resounded through the dust as flashes of light painted the walls with yellow. She collapsed, blood spreading across the floor. I kept shooting. If Elijah was gone, she shouldn't be here either.

The gun clicked.

I kept pulling.

In the aftermath, I picked up my shell casings and concealed anything that may betray me. I left. Snuck out of the house and circled the block to where my car was waiting. I climbed inside.

My head swam. I was dizzy with what I had done. I'd never killed anyone before. Didn't even know I could, if I was being honest with myself. And it was here, now, sitting in my car, knowing I could barely walk, much less drive in my current state, that I allowed myself to cry. After four days of watching and waiting, my earbud radio always switched on, always in place, just in case, I finally succumbed to the truth. I was finally honest with myself.

Elijah was gone.

18

The blistering sun gave no reprieve. Night was some illusionary stranger who didn't seem to know these endless wastes, or maybe didn't care enough to get acquainted. Cover, as little as there was, offered its strange sensation. There were no shadows here, and yet, under cover of ruined pillars and ancient buildings, it felt cooler. As though there ought to be a blanket of silhouette, but it had forgotten to arrive. The shadows were late to work.

"Shadow." I prod deep inside of myself to find him, whose voice was now a quiet whisper in my soul. He had nowhere to live, no night to stretch out into, so he had coiled inside me like a spring. It was uncomfortable, but I dare not think of the alternative.

I am still here, Elijah, he said. His voice was like rice paper held over an open flame: ready to burst.

"Just hold on. We'll find something soon." It was a lie. An honest lie, but a lie all the same, and both he and I knew it.

How long had it been? Days? Weeks? The sun never set, rather moved endlessly around the sky in a halo. I thought back to stories I had heard of summers in the far north. The sun dipping momentarily behind clouds and mountains to give gentle darkness to those that lived there, only to reemerge moments later just as blinding. Here, however, there were no clouds for the sun to play hide and seek, and the only mountains we saw were made of sand, piled high above us like waves.

I hadn't slept since our arrival, and Shadow's power, dim as it was in this Hell, kept the worst side effects of deprivation at bay. Still, not all ailments are physical, and it was because of this that I ignored the scatters of white that flitted across the sands, moving to surround us. I saw them, of course, their undulating forms some of the only variance of this ocean, but I dismissed them for what they were. Mirages. Hallucinations. Even when one of them shot straight for me and wrapped itself around my feet like some sort of holy bond. Even when it spoke to me.

You bring a Shade into the Glintlands, I imagined it saying. *Who are you? How did you arrive?*

Of course, the only logical thing to do was ignore it. The moment I respond would be the moment I admit my lunacy, and I would not allow the sun to claim victory over my mind. Not yet.

We were Folded here by a Glint in the Overworld, Shadow said.

I stopped moving. Had Shadow heard this light talking too? Or was I imagining his words as well? If so, how long had I been hallucinating Shadow? Was he already dead? Had he always been dead?

What is your name, Shade?

What is your name, Shadow? I know you have one, but you've never told it to me. Kept it secret. You've only ever said to call you Shadow. If this were really happening, and not just figments of the heat's inflicted lunacy, whatever his answer is may prove it.

Arystic the Cursed, he said, followed by gasps from the scattered lights.

Arystic? What a silly name. Not even during fits of hysteria, with the devil of insanity knocking on my door, could I come up with such a name.

So, reality it is. Alright, then. A question for the dazzling lights.

"What are you?"

19

The sun glared between towering buildings. Beautiful shadows held firm to their casters, leaning backward with outstretched arms as though afraid to fall into the pit of light. Scattered debris and well-nourished metal bins littered the filthy space between towering concrete and glass. The air hung thick with suffocating heat, and the sun's apex ensured humanity no reprieve.

Folded space like intricate origami pulled the world to a point before dispelling the Glint onto the grime-covered concrete. She writhed, stretching her tendrils of light towards the sky, filling the alleyway as she inhaled.

No going back again, she said. *Not after that.*

The Glint coiled herself, twisting and folding into a shape no bigger than a fist. Small enough no human would see her, especially in the light of day. With her newfound freedom, she flitted across the ground, exploring the Overworld city.

Where did I emerge this time? She asked, soon coming upon a lush green oasis in the middle of the manufactured maze. *And how is it that after a hundred years I still find such foreign places? A garden in the middle of a city?*

To the common human, the Glint appeared no more than the illumination from a cracked flashlight lens. Scattered, fleeting tendrils of rainbow flavored diffusion across the daylight bathed floor. Yet those that looked for the invisible could sometimes glimpse the array of beauty, as was with the young Johnathan Crow, who sat alongside his mother periodically licking a fresh lollipop. He spotted the kaleidoscope of color sprawled across the grass and stared, mesmerized by its dance.

So, the Glint danced, and Johnathan's eyes followed. She strayed too far from view. He went after her. As the sun began to set behind the buildings, their long shadows like fingers grasping to strangle the light, the Glint finally noticed the young boy. She fled, searching for a safe harbor. Johnathan Crow followed. She dodged him, darting away into the ever-decreasing bands of yellow, knowing that if she couldn't find somewhere to survive the night, the darkness would take her completely. Johnathan Crow followed.

Damn humans, she said. *I cannot flee from the night as well as a child.* She flipped herself back and raced toward the boy, rising like a wave amidst the grass. Johnathan smiled wide, dropped his swirled candy and stretched out his arms, awaiting the Glint's embrace. She reached out with a tendril and tapped him on the head.

He Folded like intricate origami, then all at once, was gone.

Finally, the Glint said, but looking around, she saw the trap she had laid herself. Closing on all sides were pure shadows as the sun finished its rapid descent. Her room of light constricted, and with it encroached her inevitable death.

"Johnathan?" a woman asked. The mother. She had rounded a tree in search of her lost son. The only evidence of which was the lollipop that lay still in a square of light.

Humans are a funny thing. They have a marvelous capacity for light and dark, each one born with a bit of both inside. Ms. Lilliana Crow held so much light, in fact, that when she stepped into the pinprick of light and crushed her son's lollipop, even the Glint could see it like a beacon shining on the shore. Her outpost.

It was in this moment that Soltr the Glint Bound herself to Ms. Lilliana Crow.

20

There was a moment after Masako. One that made me believe in some higher power: *God*—if the humans were to be believed. Masako pierced her body with her husband's blade, and I was sent adrift in the ether, awaiting my next bind. Only this time, it didn't come. For two full hours, across the entire planet, no human was born.

A few confusing seconds passed before I realized what was happening. With no new humans, I was untethered, unbound, so I took my opportunity to explore. The world had changed over the last nine lifetimes. Weapons had been created, people had been genocided, and humans had grown to be one of the most disgusting things I had ever seen. I had started to enjoy their taste, sickening as that sounds. I scoured the world, flitting through shadows and experiencing everything I could while my freedom allowed. I was in search of something Masako's sacrifice had drained me of. Hope.

Shades are incredibly fast. What humans experience, we can experience at one hundred times the speed. Maybe more. One of the atrocities of my curse was being forced to move and experience the world as they did. Like living through thick honey. Therefore, I was a bit out of practice when it came to moving at my speed, and it took some work to ramp back up to a pace I would have once considered meandering. Even so, I saw much more in my time than many humans could in their entire life, and you know what I learned? Or, rather, what idea was reinforced in my mind that day?

Humans are monsters.

There isn't one among them that wouldn't sell their own family away for money or fame or power, and there certainly weren't any that fought against injustice, not really. There wasn't a single human alive who wouldn't take the power that I would give them and use it to fulfill their own egotistical desires. I could not, in one hundred times two hours, find anyone that gave me hope because of one clear truth; there was none to give.

Hope was dead. Suffocated by the disease that is humanity and its constant desire for power. Masako had taken any hope this world could possibly have to offer and plunged a blade into its stomach.

21

They brought us into a building. It felt like a contradiction to the Glintlands' nature. A structure under the sands in a world where light permeates everything, and even down here, hundreds of feet below the dunes, light shone as though the sun itself sat as a chandelier atop the high ceiling. Yet, the room was cool. Damp. For the first time in eternity I felt cold, and I shivered in the sunlight.

Glints, at least that's what Shadow called them, wait, no, Arystic. That's what Arystic called them. They flooded this grand room, flanking the walls like sentry guards at their posts, and, placed evenly, they created a path between them. A path which led to a Glint that towered hundreds of feet above me, sitting atop a throne fit for someone their size. A King.

Kneel, Arystic said. I dropped to one knee and bowed; no use arguing with him on matters I know nothing about. Those that had ushered us in knelt as well, their many tendrils bowing forward, cresting in the back like tumbling ocean waves.

Who are you? the King asked. *And how is it that you have come to be in our presence?*

"We–"

We were Folded by a Glint, said Arystic. *One who has bound herself to a human of her own.*

Arystic had told me a bit about the Glints on our way here. They and the Shades were two diametrically opposed forces, like yin and yang. Through Arystic's extended time with humans, he had learned to sort of mimic our faces, which made talking to him easier. More familiar. These Glints had no need for such tricks. Their bodies of pure white rainbows held no human features, no faces. Which is why, when I felt the King's eyes staring through me and at Arystic, ignoring my existence altogether, it was all the more disconcerting. Like being in an empty room and becoming aware of the walls' sentience. Like nakedness. Like Shame. Only, deeper.

You, the King said, *were sent here by Soltr.*

It wasn't a question.

"Who is Soltr?" The look given to me by the faceless wall let me know I spoke out of turn. I was not permitted to speak. I was simply a grain of sand caught between two clashing waves.

What is she doing in the Overworld? Arystic asked. So that's what they called earth. *Was she Cursed to be Bound as I was?*

No. These beings do not speak. I feel their words in me, like a radio frequency that only my brain can tune to. Yet the King's voice was so powerful, the walls of the room shook, and waterfalls of sand cascaded down their surfaces. *Like you, Arystic the Cursed, she yearned to explore the Overworld. We discovered her betrayal and laid a trap for her next return. She was to be fed to the Maw.*

A mercy, considering the crime.

Yes. We laid in wait for days, but she never returned. She had Bound herself to a human to stay alive. The way he emphasized *human* made it perfectly clear what he thought of my kind. We were like insects. Rodents. Invasive creatures better killed than let live. I couldn't imagine how infuriating it must have been for him to speak through a human in this moment.

Then it dawned on me. And I smiled.

"How do we get out of here?" I asked.

Elijah...

"No," I said, then turned my attention to the King. "I can understand perfectly well what you think of my kind, and it seems you aren't very fond of Shades, either."

Yet you speak still. The waterfalls flowed.

"Because you want something from us."

If a faceless, featureless wall made of pure light could scoff, He did. The sound was like radio static. It tickled my brain.

"If I am wrong, then why are we still alive?"

Silence. Undulating Glints froze in place, and I was the only one who dared breathe while waiting for the King's response. Perhaps I was the only being in the room that needed to breathe. An interesting thought.

Soltr, He finally said, to Shadow of course, *cannot remain in the Overworld. She corrupts it the very same way you once did, only she has not taken the Curse, as you have.*

What does that mean, exactly? Good. I wasn't the only one confused by this King's cryptic bush beating.

She has Bound herself out of necessity, unable to survive during the Overworld's night. However, she can unbind herself at will, and roam freely if she wishes. She will continue to wreak havoc while she remains free. I fear the Maw's awakening in response to her freedom.

"So what? You could teleport to Earth just like she did, why not go after her and force her back here?"

And expedite the Maw's awakening? You know nothing, human. Now cease your chatter.

"You need our help," I said. The wall grew silent and shook with rage. "Why don't you swallow your pride and ask us what you've been wanting to ask us since you heard of our arrival in the Glintlands."

In the five years I had known Victoria she had taught me a great many things that I had missed growing up a hermit. I had even gotten my GED two years ago. Hated every second of it. One of the more important things she taught me was how to gamble—how to read faces, speech, body language. I learned how to read a room. How to know when you've lost, or when you've won, and when you have all the cards. That's where we were in this very instant. I had all the cards. All the power. Glints may flank me at every side, and a King the size of a skyscraper may lord above me and despise me with every fiber of his lustrous being, but I had won. I had won the second we entered the room and the King decided He needed me.

I was mightier than a king in the land with no shade.

You can kill her, He said.

What? How? If Arystic was upset at my risk, he did an exceptional job at hiding it.

She is Uncursed. If you kill her Bind while she is still Bound to it, she will die with it. He spoke as though reciting from a rule book. *Furthermore, your Curse does not seem to upset the Maw. You have roamed the Overworld for nearly a millennium, and the Maw has not so much as stirred. You also know Soltr's Bind, so you need not search for long. In many ways, you are... uniquely suited for the task.*

"What do we get in return?"

You get my mercy in that I do not kill you here and now.

No. Elijah is right. What will you give us in return?

I couldn't help but feel elated. Arystic stood by me against forces I didn't understand. I stood in the presence of what are essentially gods and making a fool of myself, and he had sided with me.

It was a small gesture, and there are a great many things that have happened since our return from the woods that could have made me feel the way I did in that moment, but this was the straw that broke the camel's back. In this moment, I finally felt love for my Shadow.

We can break your Curse, the King said.

"What?"

What?

We can break your Curse. Once Soltr is dead, and her light extinguished, we will lift your Curse, and you may roam the shadows of the Overworld forever.

But, the Maw...

Will not aim Its wrath at the Glints if It awakens to your interference. You could even be free to return to the Shadelands if that is what you wish. Now, do we have a deal?

A life without Shadow? What would that even be like? Freedom, a normal life, no more hunger.

Solitude.

Deal.

"Shadow?"

In the next moment, we were pulled through space by a puncture. Pinched and spiraled through time in one precise point. Folded like origami. Then, the blare of a horn and screech of tires as my shoes hit solid ground on the familiar Manhattan streets.

Shock

22

Stories are many splendored things. They establish characters, plots, tensions, and perhaps, most importantly, they remind their readers what it's like to feel. Sorrow, heart break, unyielding love, immeasurable joy, and the wide gambits between. Some stories, if they are written well enough, can even let their reader know how it feels to die. What is truly magnificent about stories, however, are their tellers. Those who choose what is told, and how to tell it. A story may take place over centuries, minutes, or even a single moment, frozen forever despite the eloquent writing, and it is here, dear Reader, amidst the chrome polished space shuttles and the overhanging biplanes of the Smithsonian Aerospace Museum's massive warehouse entrance, that we focus on one of these moments, seared forever in the minds of those who lived it.

It was long after closing; cleaning staff and employees responsible for locking up for the night hadn't set foot on the carpet paneled flooring for several hours. No clouds obscured the sky from view, and the lack of the moon's vibrance left the night in an ominous darkness that bled into the museum's front and skylight windows, abated only every so often by dim security lights spaced too far apart. The warm stone walls of the room, broken in half by a second story balcony, surrendered their usual welcoming nature and stood as dark judges over the room's occupants. The scene held a great many things, all with their own stories to tell, but in the end, everything in the room was... despite.

Yes, that's a good word for it. *Despite*. The night was darker than usual despite the clear sky. The walls adopted their judgements despite their usual warmth. The room held two occupants despite the hour.

Two occupants. A man and a woman. Who, just seconds before our frozen moment, had crossed deserts and timelines and locked Smithsonian doors to see each other after years of longing. Years of waiting. Lovers. Their hearts paused; skipping beats long before our moment. Here, only a few feet from each other, with arms outstretched but yet to embrace, our lovers met again despite all that had kept them apart.

This would be the last time they would be happy, despite their immeasurable joy.

They stood in stark contrast. Victoria in her tall heels and silver gown with no shoulders or back, and Elijah who, quite literally, hadn't changed clothes in four years. Grime, sweat, and an unending amount of sand, stained and poured off his skin and tattered garb. If we were privy to the smell of the scene, it would be far from enjoyable. Still, there were similarities between the two as well, and their feelings of relief at the mere sight of one another was enough to sway the surrounding stone-walled judges. The darkness was pushed away in lieu of the kind, spiritual warmth that only comes from love strong enough to become palpable. The last thing they shared only just presented itself before our story's pause: surprise. Eyebrows slightly risen, jaws let loose on their hinges, and eyes growing wide as their smiles stood one breath from fading.

The last thing in the room this night was a spear of shadow that connected the two lovers. It had only just spawned from Elijah's chest before this moment, shooting through air, cloth, and flesh, stopping as soon as it started, with its point protruding through Victoria's exposed shoulder blades. The last despite. The despite of Elijah's Shadow killing the woman he loves more than himself with no warning. No reason. The hardest despite in the room.

Storytellers make a choice how to tell their stories, dear Reader. They control whether a story takes place over centuries, minutes, or even one, infinitely long moment. I know how this story ends. I know that once this moment is unfrozen, and Elijah and Victoria are allowed to breathe once again, there will be nothing but death and sorrow and heartbreak for a long, long time. But in this moment, they are happy, and they are the closest they will ever be to each other in life ever again.

23

Have you heard it? The rumblings in the deep? Like fettered Chaos breaking its chains. The earth is splitting, unleashing torrents of its energy with every quake and shiver. The insects have heard it; It crushes them while they crawl across the land. The birds have heard it; It clips their wings as they flit through the sky. The fish have heard it; It suffocates them as they swim through the five oceans.

Deep beneath the surface Its behemoth body tears the earth asunder, granting Its own sweet release. Its body of rotating tendrils breaks free from Its prison of barnacles, coral, and earth like winding sawblades, consuming all in Its path. Not for want, nor hunger, nor desire, but because that is Its nature. It consumes. It rises now after untold eons because something, somewhere, calls to It. Calls Its ancient name, beckoning It from the depths. A perversion of the balance It once established.

The Maw has awakened.

24

Elijah worked the shovel in front of his headstone. With each grunt of force, new ground flew from the shallow grave. It had been an hour at this point, the rain both helping to soften the ground and hindering his cold, wet body. He did not slow. He did not pant. His eyes were firelight, drawn close in a rage that burrowed deeper with every pile of earth he flung over his shoulder. He was forced to stand up and look at the plastic covered body with each heave before ducking back down into his hole.

Elijah... Shadow said.

His pace quickened. The voice of his betrayer gave him renewed vigor. How dare Shadow speak while the fruits of his labor slept lifeless in the plastic. How dare he still be bound to Elijah after what he did.

Elijah, please... he tried again.

"Shut the hell up."

Elijah dug for another hour to finish the grave in silence, his rage churning beneath his skin. He pulled the plastic mound down into the grave, which landed with a thump, settling into an awkward twist. Elijah bent down and hefted the body, making her more comfortable. He could see Victoria's face through the layers of plastic.

He climbed out of the grave and began the work of filling the hole, a much faster process than its predecessor. Halfway through, Shadow spoke again. Four words, each one searing itself into Elijah's memory like hot iron to hide. With these words, Elijah swore he would never let Shadow leave.

Not until he killed him.

I had to, Elijah.

25

Fine, I said. *Your theory was correct. I cannot leave you, and I cannot hurt you. Happy?*

Two years. It had been two years since I had left on that hollow threat, and what had the Bind done? Nothing. He sat exactly where I had left him. He did not move, did not eat, did not react. Father of Shades, he did not fear. The hunger reared its ugly head after only three months, and he just sat there, patient. Content in the knowledge that the hunger would hurt, but he would not die. I had grown tired of waiting for him to herald my return. I was hungry too.

"Why?" he asked.

Why what?

"Why can't you hurt me? And why can't you leave me? And why did you choose me?"

Do not think for a second that I chose this, Bind.

"Elijah."

What?

"My name is Elijah. I want you to call me by my name. Please."

Please? Two years in the woods with no food, and the Bind was like some sort of sage. He was polite, he no longer rambled, at least not as bad as he used to. What had happened while I was gone?

... I cannot hurt you... Elijah... because I would only hurt myself as well. It is part of my Curse, the same one that Bound me to you when you were born, and that keeps me from leaving you until you... die. Was that too much? Was the concept of one's own mortality too much for a thirteen-year-old? Why do I care?

"How did you get cursed?"

I am not a stranger to these questions. Many of my Binds ask them, but usually not for several decades. Not until their lives are spent and my powers have granted them their vanity. I used to simply tell the truth. That changed after Ira. However, now, hundreds of years later, I am compelled by a child to break my vow of deceit, but the whole truth would probably go over a child's head.

I loved what I should not have, and that must suffice.

Silence. I could sense my darkness coil like a spring, ready to take flight. Tension. It is as though the forest held its breath for the child's answer. I know I held mine.

"So, what do I call you?" he asked. Just like that, the tension subsided. It breathed. I breathed.

Call me Shadow.

"Is that your name?"

No, but I prefer it.

"Why?"

... Reasons.

"Okay. Hi Shadow, I'm Elijah, and I forgive you."

I thought back to all the wrong I had done to him. Forcing him to eat humans, killing his parents, leaving him in the wilderness for years, all of which would justify any human's wrath.

For... which part, exactly?

"All of it, of course."

Lightning curled the war-torn sky, reaching out in violent plumes of yellow-white screams, creating chaotic rhythm. The clouds above wept as they witnessed the struggle between Bind and Shade. A lone peak of earth gave them their arena. Their echoing stumbles and screams drowned by the storm as the Maw watched, their private audience on the throat of the world.

The Bind peeled his Shade from the floor. Its body, thick and thinner than paper, flowed through his fingers like bed sheets. He loomed the darkness, building it into a heap in his arms as it tried to crawl away.

Why? it screamed. *Elijah, please. Do not do this.*

"You took her from me," said the Bind, his wet beard buzzed with his words. "You deserve to die!"

With a heave he gathered the last of the sprawled Shade in his arms and struggled toward the cliff's edge. The Maw creaked open its mouth, and light spewed forth. It surfaced from the world like a breaching whale ready to devour the sun. It awaited its meal.

The folded Shade, its top half spilled over its Bind's arms, whipped up and dug its teeth into Elijah's fleshy shoulder. Jagged red light broke across the Shade's skin, matching the fresh marks it had given its Bind. Lightning struck in parallel with their screams.

The Bind tore his Shade's mouth free, hurling the dark cloth away. It struck the stone with a wet slap that could have been thunder itself. The Bind staggered over to its face, curling his hands around its proverbial throat. Where once his hands would have fallen short, or even through, now they interlaced like vines, constricting the Shade's body and pushing its very being above and below his clenched fists.

The Shade pulled its body close and swept its Binds feet from under him. Sideways, the man fell, releasing his grip and smacking the stone floor below. His head bounced twice from the impact, and he laid still next to his shadow.

The Maw, eagerly awaiting its dark morsel, withdrew disappointed.

27

That was close, Soltr said. Her fractal form had leapt from Lilliana the moment her demise became inevitable. Moments later, the crack of fire and the crumpling of flesh signaled the death of her once Bind. Soltr knew the rules.

It was only a moment before Soltr chose her next Bind. It wasn't a hard decision, simply one made of necessity and opportunity.

Soltr bound herself to the murderer.

To Victoria.

28

I wake to rain pattering upon my face. How long had I been unconscious? Doesn't matter. The world is still chaos. Only... the Maw was gone. It no longer breached the earth with its gaping mouth, waiting for me to throw Arystic into it.

Arystic.

I struggle to my feet. White-hot pain pinches my shoulder, and I instinctually grasp it. Slumped, wet, and finally coming to, I remember the events of the night. The Maw's awakening, my fight with the Shade, him biting my shoulder, all of it. I had held onto him from the moment he killed Victoria, refusing to let him leave. I had trapped him. Now... now he's gone. The endless, sleepless nights to force our bond after the curse had been lifted, the discovery of where to find the Maw, and when it would awaken, the justice I had planned to serve, it was for nothing. It was over.

I had lost.

My only hope was that the Maw had devoured Arystic the Shade while I had slept.

I began down the mountain. Alone.

Aftermath

29

Elijah.

"Yes, Arystic?"

Please call me Shadow. I have not gone by Arystic in centuries.

"Ever since Masako gave you the name?"

Yes.

"Very well, what is it, Shadow?"

How could I tell him? How could I explain this?

Once we find Lilliana, and kill her, the Curse will be lifted. We will no longer be Bound.

"That's the deal you made, yes. What are you getting at?"

I have a... request. If I were human, I could have taken a breath. Calmed my nerves. *Without the Curse, if I Bind myself to someone, and they die, I will die with them. At least, that is what King Iritas said would happen to Soltr.*

"Right?"

When the Curse is lifted, you will be free of me. You will live a normal life free from our hunger, and many more things. You will grow old without me, but with those that you love, without fear of what I may do to them. I know this is what you have wanted for a long time. But when it is your time to pass, when you sit old and dying... this was it. The important question. Asked while driving in a taxi through the streets of the city, on our way to be reunited with Elijah's Victoria in a museum. *Will you let me Bind myself to you again? Will you let me die with you?*

Elijah was quiet the rest of the way to the museum. I had no idea what went through his mind, but I could imagine. Why grant me this mercy? After what I had done to his parents, how I had forced him to grow up, forced him to live? I was a monster. Why show me kindness when it was not requisite?

"Shadow," he said. I prepared myself for the inevitable no, under no uncertain circumstance, never. "Of course I will let you Bind yourself to me and die, even if I have to crawl to you."

Are you... sure?

"If it is your wish, I would love to grant it."

The vehicle stopped in front of the aerospace museum. We were here. And we were happy.

The young Jefferson was many things. Handsome? Of course. Though the only ones who said so were family and friends come to coo over the fat-filled cheeks of the nearly-one-year-old. Thin? Most definitely. Even now, one could tell he would grow to be a gangly thing, especially in his teenage years, but there was hope that he, like his father, would fill out by adulthood, cutting quite the figure. Above all, however, more than his charm or inevitable collection of broken hearts, the young Jefferson was smart, and as is the way for smart children, the young Jefferson enjoyed getting himself into trouble. Now, as he climbed the cabinet drawers to the countertops while the phone momentarily took his mother's focus away from scrubbing dishes, he was doing just that.

"Jefferson residence, Lyla speaking. Oh, hi honey." The young child paused for a moment, one leg poised to lift himself higher. He sat bewildered. It was only nearly four in the afternoon, and his father was not due home again for another several hours. What would possess him to call? Curious.

He continued his ascent.

"That's wonderful news, honey." Mrs. Jefferson said, the rapid tapping of her feet matching her excitement. "When can we expect to see it?"

Young Jefferson clambered over the last drawer and onto the countertop. The last drawer gave a shake, clattering its contents inside. He waited for the inevitable investigation, the scolding and immediate coddling of an all-too-innocent, all-too-smart, young boy, but it never came. So preoccupied with her husband's news, Mrs. Jefferson did not hear the drawer's clattering contents, nor the tiny wet padded footfalls of bare feet on wet countertop.

Up here, young Jefferson could see everything. Their kitchen table and its three wooden chairs, the double sofa sitting only a few feet from a television smaller than he was, even the hard-tiled floor far below, which he saw as he teetered on the rounded wooden edge. A strange feeling he did not yet recognize as vertigo swam through his head.

Despite his intelligence, one of the great many things young Jefferson still didn't know was that water, especially when mixed with soap, was something that made many a surface slippery, and there, as he teetered on the edge of the kitchen's mountain, staring at the white pool of tile far below, his foot twisted from beneath him, and down he went tumbling.

Of course, smarts and good looks were not the only advantages young Jefferson had, and as the floor came rocketing toward the young boy's face, his Shadow reached out and touched the ground first. Arystic's body, like tendrilled fingers, cushioned the boy's descent, turning the plummet into a gentle feather fall. Arystic even went so far as to twist the boy so little Jefferson could land on his feet.

A squeal of delight and wonder left the child's mouth as his Shadow wisped back into form across the kitchen tile. Mrs. Jefferson came in to see her son on the floor, safe and sound, and a series of recently opened step-ladder drawers and cupboards at his side.

"Elijah, were you climbing the cabinets again? We've told you not to do that anymore, honey." Mrs. Jefferson pulled her son high into the air and jutted out her hip to give him a place to sit.

Young Jefferson, higher now than even the counter could take him, no longer cared for the sights of their apartment, the wooden chairs or double sofa. No, instead, as he ascended high into the air to be placed on his mother's hip, he cared only about the ground where he had been standing, and where the strange tendrils had saved his life. Their first selfless deed in over three hundred years.

Have you ever sat alone on the eve of an important day, with nothing but your thoughts? Life jaunts on as you sit there as stone, and an unparalleled calmness washes over you. Perhaps you sit in meditation, or, like me, on a soft cushioned armchair with lilts of music that fill the air and dance at the edges of your thoughts. The worries of tomorrow's vital, unavoidable tasks somehow slip your conscious, and you are given the purest moment of bliss one can experience. There is, truly, no greater peace.

Elijah? a familiar voice asked. I opened my eyes to see him standing in front of me, the evening light casting its long shadows, inviting him in. He was old. Tired. I had never noticed it before, though now it was unmistakable. A recognition only to be gained when one becomes old and tired themselves, it would seem.

"Hello, Shadow," I said. My smile was unavoidable at seeing my long-lost friend. I had been so worried he would not make it. "It's been a while."

Too long, he said, and a smile of his own touched his voice.

"You're cutting it close, you know."

I was not entirely sure you would want to see me again. After the mountain.

My memory flashed to the scene. The open-mouthed Maw awaiting its sacrifice. Shadow and me, fighting. The hate. The searing hot pain that still scarred our shoulders. Oh, how I've regretted my actions that day.

"Please, forgive me. I was young and angry and new to freedom."

There is nothing I have not already forgiven.

My smile returned. I had missed him. I remember how much I despised him, wanted him out of my life, but I hadn't considered just how lonely my life would be without him. I thought marriage would replace him, or children, and while I loved them all with my whole heart, it wasn't the same. They were wonderful peripheries, but peripheries all the same. Shadow was a piece of me, a part of my soul. He could not be replaced. Only missed.

"You're sure this is what you want?" I asked. "There's no guarantee it will work."

Soltr did not return after... what happened. He spoke carefully, which I appreciated.

"You must admit this circumstance is different."

True, but I would rather risk being Bound for another one hundred lifetimes for the chance at a peaceful death. His surety was reassuring.

"In that case," I said, "you have an enthusiastic invitation to join me tonight."

With that, I felt Shadow's familiar coil wrap around me, linking my soul to his. The hole at my core flooded with his cool embrace. We were Bound. Once a strange definition, but now I understood there was nothing else that could describe our link. Our Bind.

I closed my eyes and leaned my head back. All was right. My family was taken care of, my soul was complete, and my music was wonderful. The importance of tomorrow could come at this very moment, and I would be content. I did not fear my responsibility. Whatever lay beyond would be welcoming to me and Shadow. And, with any luck, Victoria would be there. I sat in unparalleled comfort, waiting for my important day.

Waiting for my death.

Chronological Order

This is the end of Elijah and Shadow's story. However, as mentioned in the Author's Note in the beginning, I've organized each story to be in chronological order. There won't be any new stories here, the content is the same. However, a new pace to the narrative, a new impact of the reveals, and undoubtedly several plotholes, can be found when reading it in chronological order.

If you wish to start, or restart, here, then thank you. And, without further adieu, we'll start our story at the beginning.

With a Smile,

Quain Holtey

Beginnings

15

It was a storm that gave birth to the Maw. An angry typhoon that called lightning and fire to scorch the earth before tsunamis buried it, swallowing it down into the endless ocean.

In the midst of this Chaos, Its form was shaped. Molded by the forces of the heavens and churning ocean. Pure energy condensed into primordial rage large enough to swallow the world. Its body was earth shrouded in black mists, and when it opened its mouth, light screamed forth in a beam that evaporated the clouds, revealing the sun once again.

But the Maw was not the only thing born in this Chaos. Flitting through this new world were beings of shadow and light that trailed across the waters. They explored their new home, living in their respective elements, circling each other endlessly, in tandem with the sun and moon.

The Maw reached into the ocean and pulled the earth back from its depths. Land flourished above the tumultuous ocean, and with it, new life. Humanity. They revealed themselves, crawling out of every cave and crevice, infesting the world like insects.

What happens next is lost to time, but what is known is that the beings of Chaos, these Shades and Glints, were separated from this earth by The Maw: given their own worlds in which to explore and make their own, while humanity was free to inevitably ruin this one. Only, they didn't. Through all their failings, the world of humanity flourished, and the inexhaustible Shades and Glints instead ruined their own worlds.

They pleaded with the Maw to let them back into the human Overworld, to let them explore beauty once again, but It refused. The Maw kept the worlds separate, saying Chaos had wrought its own demise, and that they should live in the prisons they had created, else the Maw would devour them, and they would cease to exist entirely.

And so, they did.

7

I hid beneath the trap door in the kitchen. The straw pierced my body as the dark tendrils of my siblings crawled across the floor above me. They whisked out candles and dampened fires, allowing the night's darkness to creep inside. In retrospect, hiding was useless. If I had known what I do now, I would have bound to the burly, bearded Timothy Upperbuckle, who lay asleep next to his wife only a room away, completely unaware of my encroaching demise.

Instead, I waited in my trap.

They had known of my escapades. It was only a few nights ago when Torlin had first witnessed my disappearance, and my answers to his questions did not satiate his curiosity. Now, he was here, leading the charge on my capture. My death.

I knew I wasn't meant to venture here, but I couldn't stop myself from Folding back, night after night, these last hundred years.

The Overworld had such incredible beauty: a moonrise over the endless patched fields of agriculture, the untainted wilds of what is now called the Americas, the ice capped mountains and endless oceans encouraging ignorance between sects of humans. Ah, humans. All the wonders of the Overworld paled in comparison to its inhabitants. Humans, who varied from infants to old men, homeless to queens, each with their own unique stories and personalities. How important they all feel their lives are. Their tiny, momentary lives amidst the cosmos. Candle lights under the unobstructed sun that waver, flicker, and die before a single day is set. Yet, each life still burned, and, for the briefest of moments, their lingering smoke remained in the memories of those closest to them. Useless. Gorgeous. What I wouldn't give to live a life full of meaning, even if it were for just a moment. What I wouldn't give to be human and live in this world without tainting it with my shadow.

The trap door flew open, and the tendrils of those I called family took me back to the land of the Shades.

9

Speak, Inebriate. May your words be sufficient to shift the mountains and change the Penumbra.

The Father of Shades stood tall on his perch, flanked on either side by my brothers and sisters whose dark shapes attempted contexture with the atmosphere. Our world was nothing like the Overworld where the humans have color and life. Here was nothing but hues of shadow. It was ugly. Unfair. A testament to the fools that called it home and refused to explore.

Why should we have to suffer in a world of drear when we can frolic in life with the humans, who pointedly ignore us? Could they even see us? Did it matter?

Why should we refrain from our desires? I asked. *Here there is nothing, an endless void for us to wither away in. Why experience no joy nor life, when there is no point in our suffering other than self-mutilation? We can indulge. Spread our shapes across the green and blue of the Overworld with no one to stop us. Live with humans rather than hide ourselves away to die.*

Abomination, one of my sisters muttered. Whispers of affirmation spread throughout the formless room. *The Maw should have its way with him.*

If it is an abomination to want more than this dementia, then I accept your praise, I said.

Tell me, Arystic, said Father, *are you aware what your meddling hath wrought? How humanity's beauty, the motivation behind your 'transcendence,' has dwindled into violence and destruction?*

You cannot blame me for their dark ages.

We can and we will! A voice grated to the Father's left. Torlin. *With your free reign, knowledge scatters for sake of conquest devoted to some fictitious higher being! Progress halted. No, reversed. So that you could fill your appetite and run amok throughout the Overworld, spreading war, disenlightenment, and disease in your wake!*

The Father recalled the synod to order: their dissensions of disgust and agreement echoed over top one another in the muted hall.

My betrayer brother was not wrong, of course. When I travelled throughout the world as I pleased, the darkness of home spread over humanity like an eclipse. Why that was, I could not say, but I refused to accept it as unnatural.

If we were not meant to spread ourselves over humanity, I said, *then we would not know of them. More than that, we would not be able to Fold freely to their world in the first place.*

The Maw places humanity in our reach to tempt us, said Father. *To give us acumen.*

Acumen? Over what? To choose to live eternities in dread and pain? To force us into misery so that we can, one day, be devoured by the Maw that gives us such divine life? I spat on the floor, my secretions swirling into the sinking void below. *The Maw knows nothing except to feed on our ignorance, and eventually our flesh!*

The uproar that followed my blasphemy was nothing short of entirely satisfying. Father stared through me in disbelief as the council members debated ways to end the suffering of their ears from my voice. Amidst the various, creative ways of ending my immortality, the consensus landed firmly on the only solution whose results were known to be permanent.

Give the Maw a meal, came Torlin's voice over the clamor.

No, said Father. He never broke his gaze from me. *Your heresy does not deserve reward in the belly of the Maw.* The synod awaited in eager silence, hanging off Father's words. I will admit, I was curious to what punishment he thought befit my crime of life and love.

You wish to live in the Overworld?

What was he getting at? *With my every being, yes.*

Then you shall have your desire. You shall be tethered to humanity. Bound. Forced to live shackled to that which you love so much. You will be Cursed to never leave their side.

Father, please, Torlin said. *You cannot reward his lust.*

He will find no such reward. His newly required sustenance will ensure his punishment. Father's smile was cruel as his gaze bore through me. *As the Maw 'knows nothing except to feed on our ignorance and flesh,' so too will Arystic be forced to satiate his appetite… with humanity's flesh.*

No... you can't. Please. But my words fell on deaf ears filled with the excitement of those I once called family.

16

The firelight assaulted the barricaded door, sending strings of light through cracks and holes which scattered across the floor. Clamoring steel and screams of death filled the air, but inside they were distant. Muffled. The Oda and Tokugawa armies had defeated us long ago, but their bloodlust motivated their current pursuit of my husband, and those kind enough to help us flee from our home were now being butchered in theirs.

"Help me with this," my husband said. He tugged at the buckles and ropes that held his armor in place. I pulled at the ties and loosened the strands, helping him disrobe. With one hand on the front chest piece and the other gripping the back edge, he stooped over and together we slid the armor off. My hand came away covered in hot crimson. The steel scales of his o'yoroi, the same ones that had ensured his victory so many times before, had crumbled under Oda Nobunaga's three thousand guns. A hailstorm of bullets had pierced and bent the now jagged armor into my husband's skin.

"Masako," he said. "There is a compartment. A hatch that will take you beneath the house. You can use it to get out of here. Remain hidden from the *Oni kuso yaro*." Every few words were emphasized by grunts of effort as he knelt and brandished his tanto, its short blade shimmering in the cracked fire light. Never used, always polished.

"No," I said. "No, I will not leave you. You and I will remain together, no matter the cost. Even if that cost is death,"

My husband nodded and placed his hand on my cheek. He smiled through his tears. "I do not deserve you. In this life, or the next."

The screams had dulled to a hum, barely audible in the back of my mind. I knelt beside Katsuyori, and we stared at each other before death. His eyes sparkled, wet with his love. A love I knew was reflected in my own. Then, the sickening sound of his rent flesh squishing around the blade of his tanto echoed between us. He pulled the blade, then handed it to me before he collapsed, dead at my feet. My vision grew cloudy and wet.

I sat up straight and held the blood-soaked blade in front of me. I pulled.

Hands of shadow flashed out and wrapped around the blade. Their strength held the blade in place, preventing me from fulfilling my promise.

"You have no say in this," I said.

Masako, please, Arystic said. *Do not do this. We can make it out of here, you and me. I can protect you; you know I can. Please do not leave me too.*

"My husband is dead. My people are dead. The time for protection is long past, Arystic. I want nothing more than to join my beloved Katsuyori. To fulfill my promise. And I will spend every waking moment from this point forward trying to if you stop me here."

You have so much more life to live, Masako.

I relaxed my grip of the blade and placed my hand along his. "My life is over now, sweet Arystic. I choose it to be so. You may keep me from dying for the next eighty years, but nothing you can do will help me live again, for I am already dead." His coiled grip loosened, and he slid back into my silhouette. I took position with the tanto once again.

"One day," I said, tears finding their way to the floor, "I hope you find someone that makes you feel as deeply as I feel for Katsuyori. That you may understand my words. I pray that for you, my dear, sweet, Shadow."

I plunged the blade into my stomach; its piercing sting a pale comparison to the pain I already felt. I pulled to the side, tearing my insides and spilling the floor with blood. Finally, I twisted the blade and pulled upward. My world went black, and the momentary agony subsided with everything else.

My suffering was over.

20

There was a moment after Masako. One that made me believe in some higher power: *God*—if the humans were to be believed. Masako pierced her body with her husband's blade, and I was sent adrift in the ether, awaiting my next bind. Only this time, it didn't come. For two full hours, across the entire planet, no human was born.

A few confusing seconds passed before I realized what was happening. With no new humans, I was untethered, unbound, so I took my opportunity to explore. The world had changed over the last nine lifetimes. Weapons had been created, people had been genocided, and humans had grown to be one of the most disgusting things I had ever seen. I had started to enjoy their taste, sickening as that sounds. I scoured the world, flitting through shadows and experiencing everything I could while my freedom allowed. I was in search of something Masako's sacrifice had drained me of. Hope.

Shades are incredibly fast. What humans experience, we can experience at one hundred times the speed. Maybe more. One of the atrocities of my curse was being forced to move and experience the world as they did. Like living through thick honey. Therefore, I was a bit out of practice when it came to moving at my speed, and it took some work to ramp back up to a pace I would have once considered meandering. Even so, I saw much more in my time than many humans could in their entire life, and you know what I learned? Or, rather, what idea was reinforced in my mind that day?

Humans are monsters.

There isn't one among them that wouldn't sell their own family away for money or fame or power, and there certainly weren't any that fought against injustice, not really. There wasn't a single human alive who wouldn't take the power that I would give them and use it to fulfill their own egotistical desires. I could not, in one hundred times two hours, find anyone that gave me hope because of one clear truth; there was none to give.

Hope was dead. Suffocated by the disease that is humanity and its constant desire for power. Masako had taken any hope this world could possibly have to offer and plunged a blade into its stomach.

"Mom, you're not listening," I said. I pinned the phone against my shoulder as my knife parted red and green spears from bell peppers. I had put this off all day, telling myself I would call once I had the patience. Had the courage. My bravery had arrived right before dinner. Maybe I just needed something to take my mind off of her while we talked. "I love him."

"And you think that is enough reason to abandon us?" she asked. Her voice distorted through the receiver. "There is more to marriage than being in love. Your father and I taught you that at least." Her accent grew thick as she raised her voice, and memories of stiff dresses and stinging hands flashed through my mind. I closed my eyes and reached for the next vegetable.

I knew she wouldn't understand. I had told Shane she was sure to come up with a litany of reasons why we shouldn't get married. I was too young, he wasn't educated, and of course...

"–he's a mechanic. He cannot make enough money to support you, let alone a family."

...he didn't make enough.

"I know what kind of man he is," I said. "He's strong, and hardworking. He cares about me, more than he cares about himself. There's no one else in this world he, nor I, would rather be with than each other."

Silence and static filled the receiver. I stopped chopping halfway through the onion. Had I done it? Had that been enough to silence her? To prove I wasn't the reckless child she thought me to be? Was it that easy?

"...Lyla, your father and I do not want this for you." The onion stung my eyes. "We want your children to have a better life than we could give you. If you marry this man, they will not have that. You will not have that."

"As long as I'm with someone that makes me happy, I don't care what life I live," I said. My chopping grew furious. How dare she insult me or my family.

"You will say different when you have children of your own."

"*If* having children," the knife cut deep grooves into the cutting board as it slammed down with my voice, "means my life will become miserable, then I don't want them—JESUS!"

Blood spewed forth from a fresh cut in my finger. No, not a cut. I had sliced clean through. The whole first joint of my finger had stayed on the cutting board.

"Lyla? Lyla you do not mean that. Lyla—"

"Goodbye Mother," I said, and hung up the phone. I found a towel and placed it over my finger, which stained the white fabric red.

The front door opened.

"Lyla, did you call your..." Shane trailed off as he rounded the door. A brief pause, then he rushed to my side. "Jesus. What happened?"

30

The young Jefferson was many things. Handsome? Of course. Though the only ones who said so were family and friends come to coo over the fat-filled cheeks of the nearly-one-year-old. Thin? Most definitely. Even now, one could tell he would grow to be a gangly thing, especially in his teenage years, but there was hope that he, like his father, would fill out by adulthood, cutting quite the figure. Above all, however, more than his charm or inevitable collection of broken hearts, the young Jefferson was smart, and as is the way for smart children, the young Jefferson enjoyed getting himself into trouble. Now, as he climbed the cabinet drawers to the countertops while the phone momentarily took his mother's focus away from scrubbing dishes, he was doing just that.

"Jefferson residence, Lyla speaking. Oh, hi honey." The young child paused for a moment, one leg poised to lift himself higher. He sat bewildered. It was only nearly four in the afternoon, and his father was not due home again for another several hours. What would possess him to call? Curious.

He continued his ascent.

"That's wonderful news, honey." Mrs. Jefferson said, the rapid tapping of her feet matching her excitement. "When can we expect to see it?"

Young Jefferson clambered over the last drawer and onto the countertop. The last drawer gave a shake, clattering its contents inside. He waited for the inevitable investigation, the scolding and immediate coddling of an all-too-innocent, all-too-smart, young boy, but it never came. So preoccupied with her husband's news, Mrs. Jefferson did not hear the drawer's clattering contents, nor the tiny wet padded footfalls of bare feet on wet countertop.

Up here, young Jefferson could see everything. Their kitchen table and its three wooden chairs, the double sofa sitting only a few feet from a television smaller than he was, even the hard-tiled floor far below, which he saw as he teetered on the rounded wooden edge. A strange feeling he did not yet recognize as vertigo swam through his head.

Despite his intelligence, one of the great many things young Jefferson still didn't know was that water, especially when mixed with soap, was something that made many a surface slippery, and there, as he teetered on the edge of the kitchen's mountain, staring at the white pool of tile far below, his foot twisted from beneath him, and down he went tumbling.

Of course, smarts and good looks were not the only advantages young Jefferson had, and as the floor came rocketing toward the young boy's face, his Shadow reached out and touched the ground first. Arystic's body, like tendrilled fingers, cushioned the boy's descent, turning the plummet into a gentle feather fall. Arystic even went so far as to twist the boy so little Jefferson could land on his feet.

A squeal of delight and wonder left the child's mouth as his Shadow wisped back into form across the kitchen tile. Mrs. Jefferson came in to see her son on the floor, safe and sound, and a series of recently opened step-ladder drawers and cupboards at his side.

"Elijah, were you climbing the cabinets again? We've told you not to do that anymore, honey." Mrs. Jefferson pulled her son high into the air and jutted out her hip to give him a place to sit.

Young Jefferson, higher now than even the counter could take him, no longer cared for the sights of their apartment, the wooden chairs or double sofa. No, instead, as he ascended high into the air to be placed on his mother's hip, he cared only about the ground where he had been standing, and where the strange tendrils had saved his life. Their first selfless deed in over three hundred years.

4

Their first meal was a rat. Disgusting. Stringy. Its meat tore and squished between their teeth. He didn't know it was wrong, or what his parents would think if they saw him crouched over the half-eaten corpse, and he didn't care. All he knew was their hunger, and how, for the first time since his birth, it was satiated. At least a little.

Shadow knew, however. He had been Bound to plenty of humans before now, and he knew their reactions to such animosity. Yes, he knew all about humans, especially how good they tasted compared to this rat. Their salty, muscle-ridden bodies, with welcoming bone handles for him to hold as he tore through their flesh. Oh, he knew. But his Bind did not. He was still too young, barely any teeth in him. Of course he didn't know what delicacies waited for them in the form of man. Even the ones that doted on his every move, cooing over their "brand new baby boy." Oh yes, they would be scrumptious, to say the least.

For now, though, this rat would have to do. Shadow could tell he wasn't enjoying himself, probably wasn't a fan of the texture, but the satisfaction of a full stomach was too much. He would not stop. The Bind was full, and he could not live without it now. None of them ever could. Soon it would be more rats, then dogs and cats. Then would be the hard times. Raw meat, but none of it fresh. All processed and packaged, sitting in cold boxes waiting to be cooked and drained of life by the very prey they would soon take, but he would have to endure it. He would still be too young for a full human.

Maybe, if Shadow and his Bind were lucky, they could find a newborn no one would miss. Or another child ready to go missing. That would be the perfect transition, though tricky, especially given how much his parents loved him. Shadow and his Bind would have had a much better chance in a foster home, or even out on the streets, but, no, Shadow was Bound to a human in the worst of circumstances: a place to call home, two parents, and soon he would have school with other impossible to devour children. Disappointing.

The Bind finished his rat, slurping its tail into his mouth, filling their stomach to bursting. It would be a month or two before they needed more, but for now, their appetites were satisfied, if not their palettes. Shadow knew his Bind wished he would never have to eat anything like that again. Some gave into the hunger, others didn't. They would go as long as possible before eventually caving to their desires. This Bind was one of the latter. It would be months before their next meal.

Poor Shadow.

11

I stood outside their run-down apartment. Peeled paint and cracked wood; thin walls muffled televisions and old ladies playing cards next door. Seven-twelve hung precarious on the door in front of me, my hand hovering inches away from the wood, ready to rasp out a knock.

Did I really want to be here? I knew exactly how this night would go. Lyla would get mad at me for speaking the truth simply because it was not what she wanted to hear. She would kick me out, her husband would protest, and we would ultimately attempt to repeat this adventure in another nine years with another grandchild. Was seeing him even worth this inevitable failure? Seeing the product of my daughter's mistakes flaunted in front of me? I turned on my heel and took one step before the door opened, revealing a smiling man in an unpressed white shirt and single looped tie, with a tattered jacket and jeans to complete his disheveled ensemble.

"Terah, it's so nice to see you," Shane Jefferson said. "Did you just get here?"

So genuine, so pleasant. Though I suppose someone of his standing had no choice in the matter. Cannot make your way up in the illustrious car repair world without licking some boots, I suppose. "Your top button is undone," I said, and stepped past him and inside.

So, this is where my daughter was living. Or rather, surviving. This single bedroom, wall stained, rat infested hell hole. "Are those cockroaches on the wall?"

Shane turned his head toward the wall so fast I heard his neck pop. Hope told me he had *snapped* his neck right then and there, and I awaited in eager anticipation for him to collapse to the ground. Alas, he turned back with a joking smile only a moment later. That disgusting, genuine smile. "I promise, Lyla and I keep a clean home. Can I take your coat?"

"Where?" I asked. The brief flash of confusion that spread across his brow would have made me laugh if not for the circumstances. I shrugged off my coat, grabbed either shoulder to ensure an even vertical fold, then horizontal over my arm. Perfect. I pressed it flat against my body. "I'll keep it with me, thank you."

"Right... well, Lyla is just in the kitchen making dinner. You can join Elijah at the dinner table while you wait."

We walked into the kitchen and dining area; the tiled flooring throughout would have elicited regurgitation had I already eaten. We walked past my daughter who, unprovoked, pointedly ignored my presence. Off to a good start I see. I sat at the head of the table and, after a moment's hesitation, draped my coat along the back of the chair. My coat was already tainted by the very air of this place, no point in keeping it off hard, stain-covered surfaces. I straightened my skirt, why I had decided to dress up for this was beyond me, and looked up to see my grandson.

I nearly fainted.

What sat before me was not a boy, but a ghoul. Skin stretched tight across bones, no meat on him whatsoever. His clothes fell awkwardly around his skeletal frame. He looked like he hadn't eaten in months.

"Gracious Lord in Heaven," I said. "Do you feed the thing?"

He averted his gaze, which somehow made it easier to stomach.

"Yes," Lyla said. Her first word to me in nine years.

"I don't believe you. Look at him! He's practically dust." I tore my eyes away from the malnourished beast. "Yet you seem to be eating well, Shane."

"Mother."

"What? I am just saying Elijah sits not ten feet from your good for nothing husband in this cramped apartment with nothing but God's grace keeping him from death, while Shane has obviously had his fill of food for a good long while. I feel the need to call child protective services on the two of you!"

Lyla slammed the knife she was holding down on the cutting board. Was one of her fingers shorter than the rest?

"You come here after nine years and not twenty seconds into stepping through the door threaten to take our child away from us?"

Just as I thought. She would get upset with me for simply speaking the truth. When will she grow up? "If that is what's best for the poor thing. Look at him!"

"You act like we don't know! He eats every day; we make sure of it. The doctor says there isn't anything wrong with his health and that he's not malnourished. He just doesn't seem to put on weight."

"I am not surprised. With the type of care you are able to afford I am sure your doctor recommends leeches."

"Okay, all right," Shane said. His arms were outstretched as though taming tigers. "That's enough. Terah, our son is not malnourished. He just doesn't put on very much fat. His metabolism will slow down when he gets older and he'll start to look as healthy as he is."

"How dare you." My blood boiled. A mechanic was going to talk to *me* as though *I* was the problem? No. I stood up and went to Elijah. "If you do not see the problem here, then you are the problem. You disgust me. Come on Elijah, we are leaving. I should have done this a long time ago." I pulled the boy from his seat. He was heavier than his frame made him out to be.

"Get the hell away from my son!" said Lyla. She was coming after me with a knife. My own daughter! What had gotten into her? Can't she see I'm just trying to help?

"Lyla," Shane said. "Put the knife down. Terah, put down our son." Reason met with insanity. As if I was going to listen to the man stealing my grandson's food out from under him.

"You have proven you cannot care for him, like I have always said you wouldn't be able to do.

You cannot care for him, cannot care for my daughter, cannot even care for yourself!"

***

Elijah cowered in fear. He didn't want to be in this stranger's arms, but he had no idea how to get out. Everyone was screaming, and he didn't fully understand why, only that it was his fault. It was always his fault.

Bind, came the familiar voice, *I can make them quiet. All this screaming can go away. Would you like that?*

Elijah nodded into the woman's shoulder. All he wanted was for the fighting to stop. For his parents to stop screaming. For the woman to put him down. If he had known what Shadow would do, maybe he could have said something, but none of the arguing made any sense. And he was just so hungry.

Shadow lashed out like quills across the room, piercing the walls, cupboards, ceiling, and people. He flattened and expanded his quills and cut through bone as easy as muscle, dicing their bodies into thick chunks. Blood sprayed everywhere, and its thick syrup dripped off the walls. The boy started to cry at the horror around him.

But the arguing had stopped.

5

Investigating Officers: Police Officer Ryan O'Conley, Police Officer Katie Haughes

Incident No.: 092831-24T-2020

Case Description: Domestic Disturbance report.

This is the official transcription of P.O. Ryan O'Conley and P.O Katie Haughes arriving on the scene in response to a Domestic Disturbance report at 4102 12th Street, APT. 712 New York City, New York 11101

P.O. Ryan O'Conley: God damn...

P.O. Ryan O'Conley coughs and gags.

O'Conley: That's rancid. Dispatch we are outside the door to apartment 712 and there's some awful kind of smell in the hallway. Do you know about this?

Dispatch: Be advised, Officer O'Conley, neighbors called complaining about the smell. D.D. was filed due to the number of complaints.

P.O. Katie Haughes: Isn't an odor complaint more suited for building management than police?

Dispatch: Affirmative, however, neighbors said they have attempted to call the landlord and building maintenance to check in on the room but haven't heard any response.

O'Conley: In this neighborhood? Lines up. Next time give us some warning, Dispatch?

P.O. Ryan O'Conley knocks on Apartment 712's door.

O'Conley: Apartment 712, this is Officer O'Conley, open up.

Haughes: Hello? Apartment 712, can you hear us? We'd like to ask you a few questions about the smell.

O'Conley: I don't feel right about this Katie. This smell...it ain't right. Something's wrong.

P.O. Katie Haughes knocks on Apartment 712's door.

Haughes: Apartment 712, is everything alright in there? Hello?

A door opens.

Apartment 710 Resident: What's all the hollering about?

Haughes: Sorry to disturb you Ma'am, please return to your apartment.

710: Disturb me? You ain't disturbing me any more than that wretched stench. Been getting worse for weeks now, and ain't nobody doing anything about it.

O'Conley: Ma'am, do you know anything about the folks that live here?

710: Sure, the Jeffersons. Shane and Lyla. They've got a little boy, too. Um...oh what's his name?

O'Conley: Have you seen them recently? Any of them?

710: Not since before the smell started. You know, I think they left for vacation or something, and left something out on the counter that's been rotting away since.

O'Conley: Did they ever talk about going on vacation? Did you see them leave?

710: Well, no. Come to think of it, they been living here for eight years, and I don't think that Shane has ever missed a day of work, even when his boy was born. That's a man who knows how to provide for his family if you ask me.

O'Conley: Thank you for your help, ma'am. Please, return to your apartment, we'll get rid of the smell.

710: Good.

A door closes.

O'Conley: Mister and Misses Jefferson, we're coming in. Dispatch, be advised we are forcibly entering Apartment 712 on probable cause of a homicide.

Haughes: What? You heard the woman; they're probably just on vacation.

O'Conley: They don't go on vacation for eight years, then they disappear for weeks without telling anyone, and a rancid smell starts coming from their apartment? It doesn't sit right with me. What if somebody's dead, Haughes? What about that little boy?

Haughes: ...Dispatch, be advised we are forcibly entering Apartment 712 on suspicion of a dead body.

Dispatch: Received.

Wood breaks and a door opens.

P.O. Katie Haughes screams.

P.O. Ryan O'Conley vomits.

Solitude

1

Hot lemon, parsley, and smoke whisk me from my half-asleep. The crackling of the nearby fire breaks through the trees. I breathe in deep through my nose, and as the cold air floods my body, the unmistakable smell of cooked fish laid under the medley of citrus and herbs feeds my lungs. I clutch my stomach as it pinches and groans. How many days have passed since we last ate? My body rises in answer to my question. A need to get closer.

Too fast. My head swims, and my vision crowds with black static. I'm not sure if I'm still standing. The sudden blast of nausea sends me spiraling into the infinite, but eventually I find some semblance of myself, and I swim back into consciousness. The static recedes to my periphery, but doesn't fully retreat, and the blood drains from my ears, giving way to the sounds of laughter now piercing the deep night, marrying itself with the crackling fire. I peek through the bushes into the warmth.

Burt tin foil packages bursting with food sit still steaming and splayed on the lap of a man. He seasons each package before handing one to his wife and one to his young son. My stomach stabs as drool drizzles uncontrolled down my chin. Maybe, if we're lucky, they'll slip to sleep soon and leave their lemon rinds and bones for us. Maybe more if the young boy doesn't like fish...

The laughter stops. It was so sudden, I look away from the young boy's tin foil package to see the mother clutched close to her husband, both staring at the bushes. No, at me. Directly at me. I look down and witness myself standing stark in the clearing, my dirt-covered body bathed in the yellow-red firelight.

The smell of food had been too tempting. I had stepped out from the bushes. My heart entered my throat, and I turned to run, but the black static's revenge was well-timed. The darkness that I had held at bay flooded my vision once again, plunging me into the void. My head grew too heavy, and I felt the dull thud of my body as it hit the ground.

"Hey!" a man's voice said, though it was muffled through the blood in my ears. He no doubt held a stick at the ready, prepared to protect his family from the mud-caked, unclean, malnourished animal that stumbled from the forest onto their perfect family camping trip. He had no care that I was trying to flee myself, that I didn't want to be seen any more than they wanted to see me. If you just give me a moment to get right, we'll leave you in the peace you desire. I'll be back for the bones.

"Here, let me help," he said. His voice cradled my head, and his arms wrapped easily around me, tugging me skyward. When had he come all the way over here? What was he doing?

"Christ, you weigh nothing," he said. "Can you stand?"

I didn't answer. Color finally peaked through my vision.

"Can you talk?" he asked. He carried me towards the fire. Its warmth helped drive away the cold with every inch, and its light cast our silhouette in a long, jittering outline.

"What are you doing, Harold?" the woman asked. "Don't bring him over here."

"Look at him, Judith. He can't even speak," he said. "Here." He tossed me about in his arms before setting me on the log next to where he was sitting, his wife half hung off the opposite side. "Take a seat here, you can have my food. I'll make myself one of the extras." He kept one hand on my back and with the other, moved his charred tin foil package onto my lap, a plastic fork stuck vertical, piercing the fish inside.

Without question, I ravaged the package. I ate the cooked halved lemons whole, their sweet-sour citrus exploded in my mouth. The fish was covered in herbs and butter, and the skin gave way to hot white meat inside. Soon, there was nothing but bones left, so I resorted to chewing them, our hunger not yet satisfied.

I dragged my two fingers along the bottom of the foil and shoved them in my mouth. The three strangers stared at me with varied expressions of horror, curiosity, and pity. Amidst the food, I had all but forgotten where I was.

"Here," Harold said, handing me a bottle of water. "You must be thirsty, too."

"... thanks," I said. I stole away the bottle and took a sip. Soon as the water hit my lips, I couldn't help but chug its entire contents. I must have been thirsty, too. Harold offered me another bottle, which I made sure to sip slowly this time. "Thanks," I said again.

"Don't mention it," he said. "What's your name, son?"

An innocent question. No harm in them knowing my name, right? "... Elijah..."

"How old are you, Elijah?"

"... What day is it?"

"The first," Judith said. "October first."

"I'm nine," I said. I had missed my birthday.

"Jesus..." Harold said.

"Where are your mom and dad?" the boy asked. I took a long drink. His brow furrowed, and his hands shook. He hadn't touched his dinner yet, and with any luck, he wouldn't touch it at all—more food for us.

"I don't know," I said. It was the first lie I had told them.

Silence descended over the camp like a blanket, smothering the mouths of the family. Had they seen through me? The fire's intermittent crackling would break the silence, but never the tension.

"How long have you been out here, Eli?" Judith asked. She looked nothing like my mother; she was tall and thick, with straight blonde hair that fell across her back, tucked away behind one ear. Yet there was something about her that reminded me of her. Tears welled in my eyes as I remembered her love, but the dry fire fizzled them before they could fall.

"I don't know," I said. "It's starting to get cold again... so maybe a year? No more than two."

"Judith," Harold said. Without another word, she was next to her husband, leaning into one another. Their soft whispers tickled the edge of my ears, but not enough to know their words.

"Here," said the young boy. He had moved next to me at some point and was extending his tin foil plate to me. "I don't really like fish."

I immediately began to devour the meal; though I knew our appetite would not be even remotely satiated.

"My name's Jimmy. I'm nine, too."

Hello, Jimmy.

"Do you like toys? I brought a whole bunch with me from home! Mom and Dad said I could play with them all night if I wanted, since we're on vacation!"

That's nice, Jimmy.

Jimmy continued talking as I ate. He joined the white noise of my chewing, the campfire popping, and his parents' whispers. I finished eating, chewed bones and all, but we were still starving. Two whole meals and it was as though nothing had changed. Our stomach still churned and tightened, and I knew exactly why. I picked up my water and sipped it carefully. I didn't want to do it. Not again. But, the hunger...

"Elijah," Harold's voice broke through my turmoil, "how would you like to spend the night with us? Tomorrow we can take you back into town and get you cleaned up. After that, we can find your parents. What do you say?"

Judith stood behind her husband, holding his hand. She nodded and smiled in agreement, my mother's love in her eyes...

One night. Our stomach twisted with hunger, churning with renewed fervor at the prospect of another meal. My shadow quivered in time. One night. It would last us through the winter, maybe longer. One night.

Yes... we could eat them all in one night.

"Yes, please," I said.

2

The last breath of fire gives me life.

I twirl and twist upward, weaving effortless through the invisible wind.

A maze creates my infinite form,

my life is my separating unconscious.

The first color I witness is red.

Life blooming forth from lifeless mounds around my birthplace.

A Shadow looms over the death dealer,

my screams are the floating nothing.

The grip of death coils around my tail.

It is not the shadow, nor his prey, but the chill of the air that cools my body.

A death quickens the longer I live,

my death is the cooling smoke.

Life is an abstract second of horror.

6

"I don't like this," the Bind said.

What did it say?

I do not care. As though its desires held any precedent to my own. *I own you. I will always own you. I give you power. Life. Do not think for a moment, young Bind, that you are not under my control, and, if I wished, I could kill you as easily as I have any of our meals.*

"I don't think that's true."

Where was this coming from? When had it grown so bold? *What spark of insanity leads you to believe such nonsense?*

"Well, we don't really get along all that well, and I don't think you would stick around if you didn't have to. You would've killed me by now, or at least run away, if you could."

The little Bind. *Perhaps I enjoy watching you squirm.*

"No, that's not it. You get hungry when I get hungry, and you're not hungry when I'm not hungry, but if you didn't need me, you could just leave me and eat someone and then come back. You wouldn't need to wait for me to be there. In fact, it's almost like you need me to want to eat someone too before you eat them, like, you need me to be okay with it. Which I'm not. I just get so hungry. If you really didn't need me, you would just eat them yourself. And..."

Proverbial God, I hate how children ramble. Still, the little Bind had figured some of it, and at such a young age. It was far from adulthood, we had only been bound for eleven years, yet already it knew more than many Binds ever cared to know. I have no doubt its mind will give me nothing but trouble if left unchecked. Why couldn't it just be normal? Bask in the power I give it and let us eat our fill instead of running its mouth on half discovered truths?

You wish to test me?

That shut the little Bind up quick. If only I could prolong the silence. Maybe I could scare him a bit...

You think I cannot leave? We will see how you do out in these woods all by yourself, Bind.

With that I stretched myself thin, fleeing into the unending darkness of the trees and fallen leaves. The forest always has shadows, even in the day. Of course, I'm not able to separate myself from it. Not completely. It is my Bind after all. But children are easy to fool. If I'm far enough away, he won't know the difference between distance and abandonment. He'll beg for my return soon enough.

I can already hear his teeth chattering.

25

Fine, I said. *Your theory was correct. I cannot leave you, and I cannot hurt you. Happy?*

Two years. It had been two years since I had left on that hollow threat, and what had the Bind done? Nothing. He sat exactly where I had left him. He did not move, did not eat, did not react. Father of Shades, he did not fear. The hunger reared its ugly head after only three months, and he just sat there, patient. Content in the knowledge that the hunger would hurt, but he would not die. I had grown tired of waiting for him to herald my return. I was hungry too.

"Why?" he asked.

Why what?

"Why can't you hurt me? And why can't you leave me? And why did you choose me?"

Do not think for a second that I chose this, Bind.

"Elijah."

What?

"My name is Elijah. I want you to call me by my name. Please."

Please? Two years in the woods with no food, and the Bind was like some sort of sage. He was polite, he no longer rambled, at least not as bad as he used to. What had happened while I was gone?

... I cannot hurt you... Elijah... because I would only hurt myself as well. It is part of my Curse, the same one that Bound me to you when you were born, and that keeps me from leaving you until you... die. Was that too much? Was the concept of one's own mortality too much for a thirteen-year-old? Why do I care?

"How did you get cursed?"

I am not a stranger to these questions. Many of my Binds ask them, but usually not for several decades. Not until their lives are spent and my powers have granted them their vanity. I used to simply tell the truth. That changed after Ira. However, now, hundreds of years later, I am compelled by a child to break my vow of deceit, but the whole truth would probably go over a child's head.

I loved what I should not have, and that must suffice.

Silence. I could sense my darkness coil like a spring, ready to take flight. Tension. It is as though the forest held its breath for the child's answer. I know I held mine.

"So, what do I call you?" he asked. Just like that, the tension subsided. It breathed. I breathed.

Call me Shadow.

"Is that your name?"

No, but I prefer it.

"Why?"

... Reasons.

"Okay. Hi Shadow, I'm Elijah, and I forgive you."

I thought back to all the wrong I had done to him. Forcing him to eat humans, killing his parents, leaving him in the wilderness for years, all of which would justify any human's wrath.

For... which part, exactly?

"All of it, of course."

Purpose

13

I weave through the equidistant ocean of weathered stones, each uniformed monolith holding secrets of names and dates in various stages of erasure. The ground mounded at regular intervals, lulling me into security with its ebbs. Flowers in variable states of decay were placed underneath the stones' protection every so often. They painted the green grass brilliant shades of pastels wrapped in vibrant paper.

I stopped. I had found them. Three barely marked headstones placed one right after the other. The first two I had expected: Shane Jefferson and Lyla Jefferson, but the third caught me off guard. It was smaller than the other two by half, and smaller than most other gravestones in the ocean. On its weathered, forgotten face, was Elijah Jefferson. Was me.

"They think I'm dead," I said.

Not much of a surprise, considering the mess of parts we left behind, came my Shadow's response.

"The mess you left, not me."

Right. Sorry. He had gotten used to saying that these last few years.

As surreal as it was to gaze upon my own tomb, it wasn't why I had come. I turned my attention to my parents and opened my mouth to speak, but nothing came out. It didn't feel quite right. Something was missing. I stumbled away and scanned the other headstones until I found the secret ingredient to my visit: two suitable bundles of flowers: one blue iris, the other daisies. She had loved daisies, that much I remember. I brought them back and placed them under their new homes, protected under stones that had never held flowers before. Perfect.

"Mom, Dad..." I said, and any semblance of the speech I had prepared beforehand was lost in a sea of salt and water. I couldn't help myself. "I'm so sorry for what happened. Please know I didn't mean it. I was scared. We all were. I didn't know what to do, and Shadow was just trying to help me. I didn't know what would happen. I didn't know. I didn't..."

Sobs overcame my words as I knelt blubbering to cold stone. No apology was enough. I had known nothing would bring them back for a long time. Our stomach growled, and I became instantly aware of how long it had been since we'd last eaten.

"I'm—I'm going back into the city. I'm turning myself into the police."

What?

"All I've been able to think about these last few years has been how to give you justice. How to honor you. But I'm the one responsible for your deaths. I killed you..."

No, Elijah. I killed them. You had nothing to do with it.

"If I'm locked away, if we're locked away, we won't be able to hurt anyone ever again."

Elijah...

"I've made up my mind, Shadow! This is the only way I can see that's right. The only way I don't hurt any more innocent people."

The silence was peaceful. Wind swept through the trees and hummed through the low stones to create a symphony of woodwind tones. My canvas coat crumpled in the wind.

I stood. There was nothing left to say. I weaved back through the headstones and their rhythmic mounds and left the graveyard. Evening turned to night, and the lights of the city supplied their own sun. I made my way through buildings and streets to the nearest subway station.

God I was hungry.

8

The train lights flickered, bathing the residents in pure darkness for second's fractions every so often. A man took up several seats in the corner farthest from us. His snores betrayed his comfort, yet were no match for the screeching metal of spinning discs that echoed off the tunnel walls.

A woman had joined us on the last stop, younger than the man by far but perhaps only slightly older than Elijah. Her hair cascaded over top her head in black curls, grouped together by some herculean bond. She was pretty, and Elijah's accelerated heartbeat and sweating palms told me he thought so as well. She had chosen a seat directly between us and the sleeping man, right across from the sliding doors through which she had entered.

Elijah himself looked worse than the man on the other side of the car, though, to be fair, Elijah had not had a chance to look human in such a long time. His unnaturally thin body, a product of my punishment, was covered by the canvas jacket. It contorted in awkward shapes, crumpled by the empty space inside. I found myself thinking of how effective a sail it would make should we encounter a strong enough breeze. His unending restlessness would send a chorus of shifting, crumpling fabric

around us. Our stomach growled for a long moment.
Louder than the snoring.

Screeching drowns all other noises as the
train once again grinds to a halt. The power is
diverted to the brakes, and the lights' flickers
become deep flashing strobes that worsen Elijah's
headache. I relish in the long dark, happy for the
opportunity to stretch, if only for a few moments.

The doors open to three loud men who burst
into the car. Despite the rows of empty seats, they
stand. Directly in front of the woman. They speak
above the chorus of snores and screeches. They
speak loud about nothing. I hate them. They make
us feel crowded.

These men need to leave. They are ruining
the peace that we were enjoying. We only have so
much of this peace left.

"Shadow," Elijah said. A warning.

I recoil back to his silhouette. In my
subconscious I had stretched away from him and
toward the standing trio. If this had been before, I
would have ignored him, but the last time I did that,
he enforced the fast. We did not eat for years.

"...where're you going, sweetheart?" one of
the men said. He kicked the shoe of the woman in an
effort to get her attention. We know better though;
We are predators too.

She did not respond, of course. Her averted gaze and recoiled posture said everything necessary. Good. Starve them of the attention they seek. They will move on.

"Hey," the second man said. "The man asked ya a question! You'd do well to answer it 'fore I make ya."

Forceful. Irreverent. Dangerous. Elijah's blood pumped harder, and the lights flickered in time. I could feel his will stretching out. Using my power to affect reality the way I once could.

"Where I'm going is none of your concern," the girl said.

Idiot. She was doing so well.

"Oh, I beg t' differ," said the second man. "Way I sees it, you's alone tonight, and there ain't nothin' more dangerous than bein' 'lone at night here in the city." She refused to answer now, but it was too late. She added fuel to the fire with her few words. It was not her fault. None of this was. It was simply the way we disgusting predators worked.

He laughed. "We'll jus' have t' follow you home then. Make sure you's safe."

Elijah stood and took steps toward the men. I was not sure if he was aware of what he was doing, or if, like me, his subconscious urged him forward.

It did not matter. I would not stop his advance like he had mine.

"Stop it," Elijah said. His voice was that of a timid mouse.

"Leave us 'lone, lad," one said.

"Yeah, let the grown-ups talk," said another.

The woman gave a look toward Elijah. Her eyes pleaded for help, but her face contorted in confusion. She could see we wanted to help, and she wanted it too, but what could Elijah do? A poor, lanky boy with a too large coat one strong breath away from sailing across the water. Oh, but she did not know.

Did not know about me.

Elijah's blood coursed through his veins with increased fervor. The lights flickered to match his heartbeat. Thump-thump. Flick-flick. His hold on me loosened, and the pain in our stomach resounded through our bodies.

"I'll tell you again," he said. His voice now filled with my power. "Leave her be."

"Who are you to tell us what to do? Sounds like you need to be taught a lesson in manners, boy." The three men walked towards us. Good. I doubt Elijah heard what they had said with all the blood in his ears, but their advancement was a universal language.

"Shadow," Elijah said. An invitation.

The lights flickered in reverse now, plunging the train car into darkness with only quick flashes of light. The men approached, and I freed myself, stretching to the size of the car, pressing against walls and windows. They saw me in the strobe, and fear engulfed their faces, but it was too late.

I struck faster than the first could scream. With one gulp, only the waist down remained, and slumped to the floor. Dark maroon scattered across the floor before I bent down to finish my meal. The second man stood, frozen in fear. I did not need to be quick with him. I opened my mouth wide and inhaled him in one bite. He was spicier than the first. Delicious.

The last managed to run to the far end of the train and cower in the corner next to the sleeping man. I pulled Elijah closer, dragging his feet across the slick metal. The last man's screams were drowned by the sound of the subway's screeching breaks. The old man slept.

He did warn you, I said, licking back my saliva. I swallowed him whole like the last one, no need for too much blood, but I savored him, crushing his bones between my teeth. He popped like a fish egg.

We pulled into the next stop as I sulked back to Elijah, our stomach now full to bursting. He filled out his canvas coat nicely, he even seemed a bit plump. The lights returned to their normal cadence.

"What... what the hell was that?" the woman asked us.

Elijah did not answer, and we joined the cool night air as the train doors opened.

12

The pianist plucked a soft song in the background of the restaurant, serenading the array of celebrating couples seated at cloth-draped tables atop velvet carpet floors. Not a child in sight to upset the atmosphere. Wait staff moved through the tables with an air of effortlessness, like rats through a maze. Except one, who, through all her mimicry, was still bumping hips against corners and trembling platters on her palm. A uniformed man came out from the kitchen as she went in. The collision would have caused quite the clamor, ruining the ambiance for many a customer, if not for the grace of the man's trained reflexes. He had been where she was at one point, and his patience was spread plain across his face as consolations spewed readily from his mouth to match her babbling apologies.

"So," Victoria said. "How long?" Her voice pulled me from my reverie. I looked back at her, body leaning over the table, her long dark hair tickling the white cloth beneath our still-clean platters. She spoke in a hushed voice, as though sharing a secret, and the sweet smell of wine drifted to my nose from her glass.

"Sorry?" I asked.

"How long have you, you know," she glanced over her shoulder. "Have you two been *together*?"

"All my life," I said. "At least since I can remember, so as early as three or so." Curious, I took a sip of her wine. Its sweet flavor of grapes and cranberries turned sour and rank in my mouth. Why would anyone drink this?

"And it's always done what you've said?" she asked.

As if I need permission to fill our stomach, Shadow chimed in. *I am not some wild animal that needs training, Elijah. Make sure she knows that.*

"No," I said. "We haven't always seen eye to eye. Also, he's not a pet. Hell, he's older than me."

"How much older?"

"God if I know. He says he's with his Binds— what he calls the humans he's linked to—till we die, and he says he's lost count of how many he's been with."

"Well how high can he count?"

I gagged on my drink.

Better watch your mouth, little morsel. I know more than you ever could.

"Yes, but," I said, moving the cup back up to my mouth. "How high can you count, Shadow?"

"What was that?" Victoria asked.

I will make us eat everyone in this restaurant if you are not careful, Bind.

"Nothing," I said, chuckling. Shadow and I had grown closer during our fast, but I think this was the first time he made me laugh.

"So," Victoria said. "This whole vigilante thing. It's new?"

"We're not vigilantes, Victoria," I said.

"Tori, please." She slid her hand over mine, and I noticed how low cut her dress was.

"Right, Tori. The other night on the subway was the only time we've done something like that, and it was the last. Those men could have people looking for them. Families, employers, whatever. Shadow and I didn't come back to the city to start eating people."

A waiter came next to our table and set up a small foldable stand to place our meals upon. Victoria and I sat up straight once again, and with agile fingers the man cleared our place holder dishes and replaced them with steaming piles of pasta and sauce. Why did they bother with the temporary clean plates in the first place? Seems like more needless dishes.

I picked up my fork and began dancing it across my meal. Victoria, however, made no such move. I stopped to look at her.

"There's plenty of good in what you did on that subway, you know." Her eyes didn't meet mine. They were distant, gazing through the floor next to my chair. Shadow writhed beneath me, and her eyes squinted for a moment, no doubt seeing the edges of my opaque overcast shifting with his movements. Few people ever noticed, but it wasn't impossible to see. If you knew what you were looking for. "I looked them up. Two of them were charged rapists, and one had been arrested before for domestic violence. His girlfriend? Her face was swollen so badly I don't think she could see when they took her picture. Broken bones, bruises all over her body... If you and..." She trailed off.

"Shadow."

"...hadn't stopped those men–"

"Killed those men," I said.

"—then I don't want to even think about what could have happened to me that night."

How does she know all this?

"How do you know all this?" I asked.

"I have connections. Listen, Elijah," she met my gaze, her eyes were firelit amber. "This city is filled with people like them. God even the Mayor; if you knew the monstrosities he's done to get back in office... I don't know what agreement you and... Shadow... came to, but people like this need to be stopped. And you have the power to stop them."

Silverware against dishes and the low drum of conversation muted the silence that followed what she suggested. A sudden clash from the kitchen erupted from behind the door, followed by a woman's familiar apologies. Whoever she had bumped into was not as understanding as the first waiter. Not one conversation was fazed, however. It had happened in another room, behind closed doors, so it didn't bother them. They simply went on eating, blissful in their ignorance. Shadow sat still, waiting for the response that was clearly my responsibility to give. He would follow whatever path I chose, it seemed.

I twisted my fork in the pasta and pulled it up to my lips as Victoria watched with bated breath. My thoughts turned to my parents. Would they have wanted something like this for their son? Would this new path Tori presented fulfill what I sought before the subway car?

"Where would we even start?" I asked, then wrapped my mouth around my food.

19

The sun glared between towering buildings. Beautiful shadows held firm to their casters, leaning backward with outstretched arms as though afraid to fall into the pit of light. Scattered debris and well-nourished metal bins littered the filthy space between towering concrete and glass. The air hung thick with suffocating heat, and the sun's apex ensured humanity no reprieve.

Folded space like intricate origami pulled the world to a point before dispelling the Glint onto the grime-covered concrete. She writhed, stretching her tendrils of light towards the sky, filling the alleyway as she inhaled.

No going back again, she said. *Not after that.*

The Glint coiled herself, twisting and folding into a shape no bigger than a fist. Small enough no human would see her, especially in the light of day. With her newfound freedom, she flitted across the ground, exploring the Overworld city.

Where did I emerge this time? She asked, soon coming upon a lush green oasis in the middle of the manufactured maze. *And how is it that after a hundred years I still find such foreign places? A garden in the middle of a city?*

To the common human, the Glint appeared no more than the illumination from a cracked flashlight lens. Scattered, fleeting tendrils of rainbow flavored diffusion across the daylight bathed floor. Yet those that looked for the invisible could sometimes glimpse the array of beauty, as was with the young Johnathan Crow, who sat alongside his mother periodically licking a fresh lollipop. He spotted the kaleidoscope of color sprawled across the grass and stared, mesmerized by its dance.

So, the Glint danced, and Johnathan's eyes followed. She strayed too far from view. He went after her. As the sun began to set behind the buildings, their long shadows like fingers grasping to strangle the light, the Glint finally noticed the young boy. She fled, searching for a safe harbor. Johnathan Crow followed. She dodged him, darting away into the ever-decreasing bands of yellow, knowing that if she couldn't find somewhere to survive the night, the darkness would take her completely. Johnathan Crow followed.

Damn humans, she said. *I cannot flee from the night as well as a child.* She flipped herself back and raced toward the boy, rising like a wave amidst the grass. Johnathan smiled wide, dropped his swirled candy and stretched out his arms, awaiting the Glint's embrace. She reached out with a tendril and tapped him on the head.

He Folded like intricate origami, then all at once, was gone.

Finally, the Glint said, but looking around, she saw the trap she had laid herself. Closing on all sides were pure shadows as the sun finished its rapid descent. Her room of light constricted, and with it encroached her inevitable death.

"Johnathan?" a woman asked. The mother. She had rounded a tree in search of her lost son. The only evidence of which was the lollipop that lay still in a square of light.

Humans are a funny thing. They have a marvelous capacity for light and dark, each one born with a bit of both inside. Ms. Lilliana Crow held so much light, in fact, that when she stepped into the pinprick of light and crushed her son's lollipop, even the Glint could see it like a beacon shining on the shore. Her outpost.

It was in this moment that Soltr the Glint Bound herself to Ms. Lilliana Crow.

"I feel ridiculous," Elijah said.

You look ridiculous. Shadow said. His throatless chuckle rose from beneath the stiff cotton and shifting suit jacket wrapped around Elijah's body.

"If I look like a fool, then so do you."

"Focus." Victoria's voice muffled into Elijah's earpiece, her short concise voice reminding Elijah how cute her anger made her. "You look great, Eli. I wish you dressed like this more often. Now please, focus."

"Right."

Sorry, Victoria.

Elijah stood up straight and adjusted his single-looped tie one final time. He was glad for the suit coat, as it hid the thin tail tucked into his waistband which poked from beneath his overlapped tie. He handed his invitation to one of the large, well dressed bouncers that flanked the grand entryway. Without a second glance at the invitation, the guard handed him back the paper and waved him in, his focus taken up by the trio of young women gowned in glitter and smokey eyes behind Elijah.

Elijah walked through the grand glass doorway and onto the marble coated floors, their swirls of black and white reminiscent of twisted taffy. Once confident he was out of sight, he pulled to the right, breaking free from the wave of nicely dressed attendees and finding shelter behind one of the stone columns thicker than any tree Elijah had grown up with. He scanned the room's various displays of ancient weapons, wax figures, and art.

"Shadow, eyes?" Elijah asked.

Don't go anywhere.

Elijah placed his hand on the pillar. A long, thin string of ink dripped up one of the grooves. The bright lights all around the main room sent scattered shadows in every direction, giving the shade plenty of room to grow.

Finally, high above the crowd, he could breathe. He bloomed across the ceiling, a flower whose stem was far too thin, and scanned the two floors below him. Humans had become one of two things: food or Binds. However, these new rules Elijah and Victoria lived by had forced him to pay more attention. Now he had to hunt for specific meals, which taught him something he hadn't had in such a long time. Preference.

Young children with red faces and dripping noses were the ones that popped nicely in his mouth. Women tended to have a nice chew, while men came with the most meat per meal. Older humans were crunchy and brittle, better as an appetizer than a main meal. Tonight, he was on the hunt for one such man in a suit with graying hair and pale skin.

Another benefit of working with Victoria had presented itself soon after they had met; they were almost never hungry anymore. Well, they got hungry, but at least they never starved.

"Any luck?" Victoria called through the radio.

Still looking.

"Still looking, baby," Elijah said. "The issue with an old white guy as our mark is that it describes most of the people here tonight."

"I know. I would have given you a scent if I had anything. Kind of difficult when he's untouchable."

"We don't blame you. No one I know could get a scent from Mayor Ellis, especially with the current measures he has undertaken."

Found him. Second floor. Staring at the vomit of color.

"Shadow says he's looking at the Pollock," Elijah said. Shadow funneled back down to rejoin his Bind. He laid flat against the floor and set himself up to mimic Elijah's movements, settling into Elijah's silhouette.

Let us go.

Elijah moved deftly through the crowd, stopping every so often to make a show of looking at the various displays. Nothing sticks out in people's minds more when the Mayor goes missing than someone who came in and went straight towards him. They climbed the slightly curved stairs, sticking to the exposed stone sides rather than opting for the red velvet carpeting draped down the stair's center.

Why do humans delight in such randomness? Shadow asked. They weaved through the various displays ranging in different sizes, from several meter-long canvases to single square foot pedestals holding ancient pottery. *I understand the beauty of color, but it loses its appeal when smashed together without thought.*

"You can see color?" They stopped for a moment to stare at a tattered bit of rune inscribed cloth. "I would think that, with you being mostly monochromatic, you couldn't see color, or maybe just everything in a red hue."

Yes, I can see color, Shadow said. His shortness could not be overstated. *It is one of the reasons I was drawn to your world in the first place.*

"What were the other reasons?" They moved to the Pollock painting, a piece that seemed to span the width of the entire floor. Lights shown directly on the painting, creating methodically placed coned pyramids.

"I see him," Elijah said. "He's reached the end of the painting, but he's about to move to another exhibit. We need to get him alone."

I must come to your aid once again, Bind. Shadow said. He slithered through the footfalls and scattered shadows of crowded humans until he reached the other side of the painting. He coiled around the mayor's leg, slithering ever upward, around his torso, and eventually his arm. The Mayor went to take a drink from his starry glass, and the glass tipped right before it touched his lips. Profanity and chuckles left his lips as champagne soaked his white shirt, and Shadow reversed his slither to rest beneath Elijah's feet once again. *If I were you, I would make my way to the bathroom before his guards seal it off.*

Elijah ducked through the crowd. He made a rather convincing show of needing to use the restroom, Shadow thought. Once through the swinging door, he made his way into one of the empty stalls, closed the door, and perched atop the toilet so he could not be seen from the gap that ran along the floor beneath the metal walls.

Three breaths later, the door swung open yet again. Footsteps pounded along the echoing tiles, then stopped.

"Christ almighty, you'd think I'd learn to control myself," the Mayor said. The sink bubbled for a moment, then flowed water. "You need to be a picture of strength, Edmond. That's what she said. I cannot maintain support if I appear incompetent."

"Shadow," Elijah said, too quiet for the Mayor to hear during his ramblings, "bring the night."

Gladly. Shadow spread like a dark puddle across the cool floor. Thin as a sheet, he covered every crevice and winding groove. He climbed the walls, sealing shut the doorway and small window that opposed each other on either side of the room. The only ways out.

"What in the hell..." Mayor Ellis said, finally taking notice of the darkening room. He turned around to gaze at the nightmare. "What in God's name?"

Shadow made it to the ceiling. He dripped over every light fixture like wet ooze, and they popped beneath his weight. The last fixture created a spotlight above Elijah's stall before it's pop plunged the world into darkness.

The creaking of metal hinges, its normal reverb absorbed by the black.

"Wh-who's there?" the Mayor asked the dark. "Show yourself."

Shadow had coated himself around his Bind like a blanket, so when Elijah opened his eyes only a few feet from the man, Shadow's own eyes stared crimson at the Major, their glow providing the only light source in this small world. They were the eyes of death. Elijah knew it, Shadow knew it, and now so, too, did Mayor Ellis.

"Are you... what is this?"

"Mayor Edmond Ellis," They said, their mouth a villainous crack of sharp teeth and ruby void. "You willingly traded weapons and drugs for money you used to fund your second campaign. Admit to your crimes."

"I-I assure you I have no idea—"

"Confess," They said, their words drowning out the Mayor's blabbering.

"I-I-I did," he stammered. Good. Quick. "Yes, I did, but once I am re-elected, I will rid the streets of New York of crime and drugs and make the city safe once again." His excuse rang with rehearsal. "It's... It's temporary."

"And what of the innocents who are to be killed with these weapons now? What of the families that will be torn apart by the drugs you supplied for them? The children who will grow up without parents? The parents who will have to bury their children?" The room grew darker as they spoke.

What started as a silent night now turned into a reverberating void, whose only salvation lay in the red glow of death's eyes and mouth.

"Th-they're... n-necessary..." The Mayor didn't believe his own words.

The eyes recoiled for a moment. They and the crooked mouth grew in size, raising high to the ceiling. Shadow was amassing himself, tearing himself away from Elijah.

"Edmond Ellis," Elijah said, "you are guilty of crimes too abhorrent to repeat. Your right to this life is hereby revoked, as you have so willingly revoked the lives of others."

"W-wait. Please, don't do this... if you kill me, you're no better!"

"True." There was a pause, and for a moment, Mayor Edmond Ellis believed his plea had struck a chord. A glimmer of hope shown in his eyes, and he uncoiled himself, "but I accepted my demons long ago."

Shadow lunged for the man. The Mayor's screams were smothered in his throat. Crunchy, just as Shadow had anticipated, though there was something else. A hint of vanilla, Shadow thought. As he ate, Shadow dripped off the walls and hid himself once again in his Bind's silhouette.

"The Mayor's guards will be waiting outside the door," Elijah said. "Tori, Mayor Ellis is taken care of, but we need a way out."

What about the window?

Elijah looked at the small window. "Not a bad idea." He pushed against it, and it opened along the bottom, its top hinges not making a sound. Hanging halfway out, Elijah realized they dangled twenty feet above the hard asphalt below.

"Hey Shadow," Elijah said, gathering himself, "catch."

Elijah threw himself out of the window.

14

Shadow pushed off the ground, launching us above the cruel wrought iron fencing. We landed with a crunch onto the leaf-covered asphalt path. The naked trees bathed the night in an ominous, monochromatic hue that would have deterred any sane person. A few steps in and I could see our destination. Its flush stone entryway stood as a ward before the cave beyond its threshold plunged into darkness.

"Sybil's cave," I said. "I wonder what she's doing here."

Living out her Poe fantasies, Shadow said. He reached out, emboldened by the endless darkness, and gripped the gate blocking the entrance to the man-made cave.

"What's that supposed to mean?" I asked. Shadow pulled the gate apart, its metal creaking as it bent and eventually snapped, sending once chained links twisting off into the night.

Edgar spent quite some time here. They found a woman's body, so he couldn't resist, really. He was always drawn to the dark and mysterious. He spent months inspired by those events. Even wrote a piece about it. Shadow slithered back to me as he spoke, tucking himself into the folds of my silhouette.

"Wait, Edgar Allen Poe? How do you know that?" I asked.

Shadow breathed a sigh, though I was entirely sure he didn't actually need to breathe. Merely a dramatic imitation. *Poe was one of my past Binds. Now, can we eat?*

I froze. Not because it was cold, though it was, and it wasn't because this new information shocked me. I froze because I realized that I never asked Shadow about his other Binds. He's been around for what must be hundreds of years, bound to different lives, and I had never once asked. Hell, I had asked him so few questions in general. I hardly knew him. Aside from our shared hunger, I was bound to a stranger.

"Shadow," I said, still unmoving. "Why are you bound to people? You've told me you're with a Bind from birth to death, but you've never said why it's like that in the first place. Are all Shades bound to humans, or are you the only one? And why?"

There was a long pause.

Elijah, he said. *You have never once prodded. These questions take time to answer, so why ask them here, on the precipice of our hunt?*

"That's not an answer."

Another sigh. *Yes, there are other Shades, just as there are other humans. Though I am the only one bound to humanity, as far as I know. And I am bound to humanity as part of my punishment.*

"Punished for what?"

For loving what I should not. Now, can we please eat?

"I'd like to know more but," I said, and started walking towards the freshly opened gate. "You'll be happier entertaining my questions when our stomach is full." I pressed my finger to my ear. "Victoria?"

"Here," she said. Her voice was muffled through the radio static.

"We're going inside. You're sure she's here?"

"Absolutely. Reports say she uses Sybil's as a kind of hideout."

"All right, we'll probably lose you in the cave."

"Be safe."

"I love you."

"I love you, too."

I moved my arms wide and bent my knees. Shadow's arms engulfed my own, giving me dark, brutish arms tipped with jagged claws. He felt like a cool blanket.

We stepped into the cave; whose damp halls echoed with each of our footfalls. Vapor from the freshwater spring inside condensed along the ceiling, which had lengthened the stalactites during their continual slow drip back to the water below. The round cave was supported by thick pillars, crowding the already small cave and sending any noise shooting back throughout the room. One of these sounds was sporadic and would have been entirely silent if not for the walls' reverb. The sound of breathing.

"Lilliana Crow?" I asked. My question repeated endlessly in the echoes.

The breathing stopped. I walked around the pillar and could hear her footfalls mirror mine on the other side.

Elijah, where is that light coming from?

What was he talking about? It was pitch black.

"Lilliana Crow, you've caused the disappearance of seventeen people over the last six years. You've stolen their belongings, cleaned up your messes, and have always remained outside the law." The sound had changed as we continued our dance. The ground beneath me shifting under my weight. Looking down, I saw the shifting floor beneath my feet. Mounds of... sand?

Elijah, the light!

Lilliana reversed her dance, stepping in front of me and stopping me in my tracks. I swiped with my claws, but Shadow had retreated, and I swung empty fists too far to reach.

"Whoever you are," she said, placing her hand on my chest, "you can join them."

The world swirled, sucking into itself where our bodies connected. I felt myself fold and contort, slipping into the void, condensing into a single point, like being sucked through a straw.

Then out again. The entire process in reverse, like stretching over infinity. The air on the other side was hot, hostile. It burned my skin within seconds. The sun beat heavy and dry over top of us, and Shadow retreated to the confines of my–

Shadow screams. I have no silhouette for him to retreat into. My own opaque shadow was gone. Shadow's screams stopped as soon as they had started, and for the first time the heft of his form dragging my feet was gone. He was gone.

Sweat poured, and I squinted my eyes in an attempt to see anything other than blinding white. Agonizing, impossible moments where all I could feel was searing heat, my body sinking into the ground, and the absence of a piece of my soul.

Eventually my eyes adjusted to the blistering light, and were met by an ocean of endless dunes.

Lost

17

Of course I followed her. She knew where he was. She did something to him in that cave. He vanished. And I needed to know.

Where was my Elijah?

I tailed her for a few days. Honestly, I'm surprised my resolve lasted as long as that. Every fiber of my being wanted nothing more than to choke the life out of her. But tonight, I broke. I waited inside her house for her return. She had stopped going to the cave since that night and started coming back home. There was a thin layer of dust over everything, as if even when she came home, she didn't touch anything. Not just the surfaces, like her sofa or the counters, but even the floor was undisturbed, as though she didn't walk, but hovered. Who was this woman?

The deadbolt on the front door tumbled to the side, and the door opened. I waited as she stepped inside and closed the door, relocking it like I knew she would. Like she had done every night she came home.

"Where is he?" I asked.

She turned around with barely a hint of surprise. Was she expecting me?

"Where's who?" she asked. She's toying with me; I know she is. But her smile didn't match her eyes. It was cocked in confusion. Suddenly I wasn't so sure. No, she was playing dumb. She had to be. She knew where he was.

"Elijah Jefferson. What did you do with him?"

Recognition flooded her face, and her smile broadened. She *was* toying with me.

"Oh, the man and his Shade," she said. She took a few steps toward me, and I drew my gun. I hadn't come unprepared. She froze, head cocked to one side. Almost like... curiosity? "They're gone."

"Gone where? What did you do with them?" I couldn't stop my voice from cracking, nor my vision from blurring. "Where's Eli?"

"It doesn't matter. They're not coming back. No one does."

Lies.

I pulled the trigger. I pulled it again. And again. Each shot resounded through the dust as flashes of light painted the walls with yellow. She collapsed, blood spreading across the floor. I kept shooting. If Elijah was gone, she shouldn't be here either.

The gun clicked.

I kept pulling.

In the aftermath, I picked up my shell casings and concealed anything that may betray me. I left. Snuck out of the house and circled the block to where my car was waiting. I climbed inside.

My head swam. I was dizzy with what I had done. I'd never killed anyone before. Didn't even know I could, if I was being honest with myself. And it was here, now, sitting in my car, knowing I could barely walk, much less drive in my current state, that I allowed myself to cry. After four days of watching and waiting, my earbud radio always switched on, always in place, just in case, I finally succumbed to the truth. I was finally honest with myself.

Elijah was gone.

27

That was close, Soltr said. Her fractal form had leapt from Lilliana the moment her demise became inevitable. Moments later, the crack of fire and the crumpling of flesh signaled the death of her once Bind. Soltr knew the rules.

It was only a moment before Soltr chose her next Bind. It wasn't a hard decision, simply one made of necessity and opportunity.

Soltr bound herself to the murderer.

To Victoria.

18

The blistering sun gave no reprieve. Night was some illusionary stranger who didn't seem to know these endless wastes, or maybe didn't care enough to get acquainted. Cover, as little as there was, offered its strange sensation. There were no shadows here, and yet, under cover of ruined pillars and ancient buildings, it felt cooler. As though there ought to be a blanket of silhouette, but it had forgotten to arrive. The shadows were late to work.

"Shadow." I prod deep inside of myself to find him, whose voice was now a quiet whisper in my soul. He had nowhere to live, no night to stretch out into, so he had coiled inside me like a spring. It was uncomfortable, but I dare not think of the alternative.

I am still here, Elijah, he said. His voice was like rice paper held over an open flame: ready to burst.

"Just hold on. We'll find something soon." It was a lie. An honest lie, but a lie all the same, and both he and I knew it.

How long had it been? Days? Weeks? The sun never set, rather moved endlessly around the sky in a halo. I thought back to stories I had heard of summers in the far north. The sun dipping momentarily behind clouds and mountains to give gentle darkness to those that lived there, only to reemerge moments later just as blinding. Here, however, there were no clouds for the sun to play hide and seek, and the only mountains we saw were made of sand, piled high above us like waves.

I hadn't slept since our arrival, and Shadow's power, dim as it was in this Hell, kept the worst side effects of deprivation at bay. Still, not all ailments are physical, and it was because of this that I ignored the scatters of white that flitted across the sands, moving to surround us. I saw them, of course, their undulating forms some of the only variance of this ocean, but I dismissed them for what they were. Mirages. Hallucinations. Even when one of them shot straight for me and wrapped itself around my feet like some sort of holy bond. Even when it spoke to me.

You bring a Shade into the Glintlands, I imagined it saying. *Who are you? How did you arrive?*

Of course, the only logical thing to do was ignore it. The moment I respond would be the moment I admit my lunacy, and I would not allow the sun to claim victory over my mind. Not yet.

We were Folded here by a Glint in the Overworld, Shadow said.

I stopped moving. Had Shadow heard this light talking too? Or was I imagining his words as well? If so, how long had I been hallucinating Shadow? Was he already dead? Had he always been dead?

What is your name, Shade?

What is your name, Shadow? I know you have one, but you've never told it to me. Kept it secret. You've only ever said to call you Shadow. If this were really happening, and not just figments of the heat's inflicted lunacy, whatever his answer is may prove it.

Arystic the Cursed, he said, followed by gasps from the scattered lights.

Arystic? What a silly name. Not even during fits of hysteria, with the devil of insanity knocking on my door, could I come up with such a name.

So, reality it is. Alright, then. A question for the dazzling lights.

"What are you?"

21

They brought us into a building. It felt like a contradiction to the Glintlands' nature. A structure under the sands in a world where light permeates everything, and even down here, hundreds of feet below the dunes, light shone as though the sun itself sat as a chandelier atop the high ceiling. Yet, the room was cool. Damp. For the first time in eternity I felt cold, and I shivered in the sunlight.

Glints, at least that's what Shadow called them, wait, no, Arystic. That's what Arystic called them. They flooded this grand room, flanking the walls like sentry guards at their posts, and, placed evenly, they created a path between them. A path which led to a Glint that towered hundreds of feet above me, sitting atop a throne fit for someone their size. A King.

Kneel, Arystic said. I dropped to one knee and bowed; no use arguing with him on matters I know nothing about. Those that had ushered us in knelt as well, their many tendrils bowing forward, cresting in the back like tumbling ocean waves.

Who are you? the King asked. *And how is it that you have come to be in our presence?*

"We–"

We were Folded by a Glint, said Arystic. *One who has bound herself to a human of her own.*

Arystic had told me a bit about the Glints on our way here. They and the Shades were two diametrically opposed forces, like yin and yang. Through Arystic's extended time with humans, he had learned to sort of mimic our faces, which made talking to him easier. More familiar. These Glints had no need for such tricks. Their bodies of pure white rainbows held no human features, no faces. Which is why, when I felt the King's eyes staring through me and at Arystic, ignoring my existence altogether, it was all the more disconcerting. Like being in an empty room and becoming aware of the walls' sentience. Like nakedness. Like Shame. Only, deeper.

You, the King said, *were sent here by Soltr.*

It wasn't a question.

"Who is Soltr?" The look given to me by the faceless wall let me know I spoke out of turn. I was not permitted to speak. I was simply a grain of sand caught between two clashing waves.

What is she doing in the Overworld? Arystic asked. So that's what they called earth. *Was she Cursed to be Bound as I was?*

No. These beings do not speak. I feel their words in me, like a radio frequency that only my brain can tune to. Yet the King's voice was so powerful, the walls of the room shook, and waterfalls of sand cascaded down their surfaces. *Like you, Arystic the Cursed, she yearned to explore the Overworld. We discovered her betrayal and laid a trap for her next return. She was to be fed to the Maw.*

A mercy, considering the crime.

Yes. We laid in wait for days, but she never returned. She had Bound herself to a human to stay alive. The way he emphasized *human* made it perfectly clear what he thought of my kind. We were like insects. Rodents. Invasive creatures better killed than let live. I couldn't imagine how infuriating it must have been for him to speak through a human in this moment.

Then it dawned on me. And I smiled.

"How do we get out of here?" I asked.

Elijah...

"No," I said, then turned my attention to the King. "I can understand perfectly well what you think of my kind, and it seems you aren't very fond of Shades, either."

Yet you speak still. The waterfalls flowed.

"Because you want something from us."

If a faceless, featureless wall made of pure light could scoff, He did. The sound was like radio static. It tickled my brain.

"If I am wrong, then why are we still alive?"

Silence. Undulating Glints froze in place, and I was the only one who dared breathe while waiting for the King's response. Perhaps I was the only being in the room that needed to breathe. An interesting thought.

Soltr, He finally said, to Shadow of course, *cannot remain in the Overworld. She corrupts it the very same way you once did, only she has not taken the Curse, as you have.*

What does that mean, exactly? Good. I wasn't the only one confused by this King's cryptic bush beating.

She has Bound herself out of necessity, unable to survive during the Overworld's night. However, she can unbind herself at will, and roam freely if she wishes. She will continue to wreak havoc while she remains free. I fear the Maw's awakening in response to her freedom.

"So what? You could teleport to Earth just like she did, why not go after her and force her back here?"

And expedite the Maw's awakening? You know nothing, human. Now cease your chatter.

"You need our help," I said. The wall grew silent and shook with rage. "Why don't you swallow your pride and ask us what you've been wanting to ask us since you heard of our arrival in the Glintlands."

In the five years I had known Victoria she had taught me a great many things that I had missed growing up a hermit. I had even gotten my GED two years ago. Hated every second of it. One of the more important things she taught me was how to gamble—how to read faces, speech, body language. I learned how to read a room. How to know when you've lost, or when you've won, and when you have all the cards. That's where we were in this very instant. I had all the cards. All the power. Glints may flank me at every side, and a King the size of a skyscraper may lord above me and despise me with every fiber of his lustrous being, but I had won. I had won the second we entered the room and the King decided He needed me.

I was mightier than a king in the land with no shade.

You can kill her, He said.

What? How? If Arystic was upset at my risk, he did an exceptional job at hiding it.

She is Uncursed. If you kill her Bind while she is still Bound to it, she will die with it. He spoke as though reciting from a rule book. *Furthermore, your Curse does not seem to upset the Maw. You have roamed the Overworld for nearly a millennium, and the Maw has not so much as stirred. You also know Soltr's Bind, so you need not search for long. In many ways, you are... uniquely suited for the task.*

"What do we get in return?"

You get my mercy in that I do not kill you here and now.

No. Elijah is right. What will you give us in return?

I couldn't help but feel elated. Arystic stood by me against forces I didn't understand. I stood in the presence of what are essentially gods and making a fool of myself, and he had sided with me. It was a small gesture, and there are a great many things that have happened since our return from the woods that could have made me feel the way I did in that moment, but this was the straw that broke the camel's back. In this moment, I finally felt love for my Shadow.

We can break your Curse, the King said.

"What?"

What?

We can break your Curse. Once Soltr is dead, and her light extinguished, we will lift your Curse, and you may roam the shadows of the Overworld forever.

But, the Maw...

Will not aim Its wrath at the Glints if It awakens to your interference. You could even be free to return to the Shadelands if that is what you wish. Now, do we have a deal?

A life without Shadow? What would that even be like? Freedom, a normal life, no more hunger.

Solitude.

Deal.

"Shadow?"

In the next moment, we were pulled through space by a puncture. Pinched and spiraled through time in one precise point. Folded like origami. Then, the blare of a horn and screech of tires as my shoes hit solid ground on the familiar Manhattan streets.

Broken

29

Elijah.

"Yes, Arystic?"

Please call me Shadow. I have not gone by Arystic in centuries.

"Ever since Masako gave you the name?"

Yes.

"Very well, what is it, Shadow?"

How could I tell him? How could I explain this?

Once we find Lilliana, and kill her, the Curse will be lifted. We will no longer be Bound.

"That's the deal you made, yes. What are you getting at?"

I have a... request. If I were human, I could have taken a breath. Calmed my nerves. *Without the Curse, if I Bind myself to someone, and they die, I will die with them. At least, that is what King Iritas said would happen to Soltr.*

"Right?"

When the Curse is lifted, you will be free of me. You will live a normal life free from our hunger, and many more things. You will grow old without me, but with those that you love, without fear of what I may do to them. I know this is what you have wanted for a long time. But when it is your time to pass, when you sit old and dying... this was it. The important question. Asked while driving in a taxi through the streets of the city, on our way to be reunited with Elijah's Victoria in a museum. *Will you let me Bind myself to you again? Will you let me die with you?*

Elijah was quiet the rest of the way to the museum. I had no idea what went through his mind, but I could imagine. Why grant me this mercy? After what I had done to his parents, how I had forced him to grow up, forced him to live? I was a monster. Why show me kindness when it was not requisite?

"Shadow," he said. I prepared myself for the inevitable no, under no uncertain circumstance, never. "Of course I will let you Bind yourself to me and die, even if I have to crawl to you."

Are you... sure?

"If it is your wish, I would love to grant it."

The vehicle stopped in front of the aerospace museum. We were here. And we were happy.

22

Stories are many splendored things. They establish characters, plots, tensions, and perhaps, most importantly, they remind their readers what it's like to feel. Sorrow, heart break, unyielding love, immeasurable joy, and the wide gambits between. Some stories, if they are written well enough, can even let their reader know how it feels to die. What is truly magnificent about stories, however, are their tellers. Those who choose what is told, and how to tell it. A story may take place over centuries, minutes, or even a single moment, frozen forever despite the eloquent writing, and it is here, dear Reader, amidst the chrome polished space shuttles and the overhanging biplanes of the Smithsonian Aerospace Museum's massive warehouse entrance, that we focus on one of these moments, seared forever in the minds of those who lived it.

It was long after closing; cleaning staff and employees responsible for locking up for the night hadn't set foot on the carpet paneled flooring for several hours. No clouds obscured the sky from view, and the lack of the moon's vibrance left the night in an ominous darkness that bled into the museum's front and skylight windows, abated only every so often by dim security lights spaced too far apart. The warm stone walls of the room, broken in half by a second story balcony, surrendered their usual welcoming nature and stood as dark judges over the room's occupants. The scene held a great many things, all with their own stories to tell, but in the end, everything in the room was... despite.

Yes, that's a good word for it. *Despite*. The night was darker than usual despite the clear sky. The walls adopted their judgements despite their usual warmth. The room held two occupants despite the hour.

Two occupants. A man and a woman. Who, just seconds before our frozen moment, had crossed deserts and timelines and locked Smithsonian doors to see each other after years of longing. Years of waiting. Lovers. Their hearts paused; skipping beats long before our moment. Here, only a few feet from each other, with arms outstretched but yet to embrace, our lovers met again despite all that had kept them apart.

This would be the last time they would be happy, despite their immeasurable joy.

They stood in stark contrast. Victoria in her tall heels and silver gown with no shoulders or back, and Elijah who, quite literally, hadn't changed clothes in four years. Grime, sweat, and an unending amount of sand, stained and poured off his skin and tattered garb. If we were privy to the smell of the scene, it would be far from enjoyable. Still, there were similarities between the two as well, and their feelings of relief at the mere sight of one another was enough to sway the surrounding stone-walled judges. The darkness was pushed away in lieu of the kind, spiritual warmth that only comes from love strong enough to become palpable. The last thing they shared only just presented itself before our story's pause: surprise. Eyebrows slightly risen, jaws let loose on their hinges, and eyes growing wide as their smiles stood one breath from fading.

The last thing in the room this night was a spear of shadow that connected the two lovers. It had only just spawned from Elijah's chest before this moment, shooting through air, cloth, and flesh, stopping as soon as it started, with its point protruding through Victoria's exposed shoulder blades. The last despite. The despite of Elijah's Shadow killing the woman he loves more than himself with no warning. No reason. The hardest despite in the room.

Storytellers make a choice how to tell their stories, dear Reader. They control whether a story takes place over centuries, minutes, or even one, infinitely long moment. I know how this story ends. I know that once this moment is unfrozen, and Elijah and Victoria are allowed to breathe once again, there will be nothing but death and sorrow and heartbreak for a long, long time. But in this moment, they are happy, and they are the closest they will ever be to each other in life ever again.

23

Have you heard it? The rumblings in the deep? Like fettered Chaos breaking its chains. The earth is splitting, unleashing torrents of its energy with every quake and shiver. The insects have heard it; It crushes them while they crawl across the land. The birds have heard it; It clips their wings as they flit through the sky. The fish have heard it; It suffocates them as they swim through the five oceans.

Deep beneath the surface Its behemoth body tears the earth asunder, granting Its own sweet release. Its body of rotating tendrils breaks free from Its prison of barnacles, coral, and earth like winding sawblades, consuming all in Its path. Not for want, nor hunger, nor desire, but because that is Its nature. It consumes. It rises now after untold eons because something, somewhere, calls to It. Calls Its ancient name, beckoning It from the depths. A perversion of the balance It once established.

The Maw has awakened.

24

Elijah worked the shovel in front of his headstone. With each grunt of force, new ground flew from the shallow grave. It had been an hour at this point, the rain both helping to soften the ground and hindering his cold, wet body. He did not slow. He did not pant. His eyes were firelight, drawn close in a rage that burrowed deeper with every pile of earth he flung over his shoulder. He was forced to stand up and look at the plastic covered body with each heave before ducking back down into his hole.

Elijah... Shadow said.

His pace quickened. The voice of his betrayer gave him renewed vigor. How dare Shadow speak while the fruits of his labor slept lifeless in the plastic. How dare he still be bound to Elijah after what he did.

Elijah, please... he tried again.

"Shut the hell up."

Elijah dug for another hour to finish the grave in silence, his rage churning beneath his skin. He pulled the plastic mound down into the grave, which landed with a thump, settling into an awkward twist. Elijah bent down and hefted the body, making her more comfortable. He could see Victoria's face through the layers of plastic.

He climbed out of the grave and began the work of filling the hole, a much faster process than its predecessor. Halfway through, Shadow spoke again. Four words, each one searing itself into Elijah's memory like hot iron to hide. With these words, Elijah swore he would never let Shadow leave.

Not until he killed him.

I had to, Elijah.

26

Lightning curled the war-torn sky, reaching out in violent plumes of yellow-white screams, creating chaotic rhythm. The clouds above wept as they witnessed the struggle between Bind and Shade. A lone peak of earth gave them their arena. Their echoing stumbles and screams drowned by the storm as the Maw watched, their private audience on the throat of the world.

The Bind peeled his Shade from the floor. Its body, thick and thinner than paper, flowed through his fingers like bed sheets. He loomed the darkness, building it into a heap in his arms as it tried to crawl away.

Why? it screamed. *Elijah, please. Do not do this.*

"You took her from me," said the Bind, his wet beard buzzed with his words. "You deserve to die!"

With a heave he gathered the last of the sprawled Shade in his arms and struggled toward the cliff's edge. The Maw creaked open its mouth, and light spewed forth. It surfaced from the world like a breaching whale ready to devour the sun. It awaited its meal.

The folded Shade, its top half spilled over its Bind's arms, whipped up and dug its teeth into Elijah's fleshy shoulder. Jagged red light broke across the Shade's skin, matching the fresh marks it had given its Bind. Lightning struck in parallel with their screams.

The Bind tore his Shade's mouth free, hurling the dark cloth away. It struck the stone with a wet slap that could have been thunder itself. The Bind staggered over to its face, curling his hands around its proverbial throat. Where once his hands would have fallen short, or even through, now they interlaced like vines, constricting the Shade's body and pushing its very being above and below his clenched fists.

The Shade pulled its body close and swept its Binds feet from under him. Sideways, the man fell, releasing his grip and smacking the stone floor below. His head bounced twice from the impact, and he laid still next to his shadow.

The Maw, eagerly awaiting its dark morsel, withdrew disappointed.

28

I wake to rain pattering upon my face. How long had I been unconscious? Doesn't matter. The world is still chaos. Only... the Maw was gone. It no longer breached the earth with its gaping mouth, waiting for me to throw Arystic into it.

Arystic.

I struggle to my feet. White-hot pain pinches my shoulder, and I instinctually grasp it. Slumped, wet, and finally coming to, I remember the events of the night. The Maw's awakening, my fight with the Shade, him biting my shoulder, all of it. I had held onto him from the moment he killed Victoria, refusing to let him leave. I had trapped him. Now... now he's gone. The endless, sleepless nights to force our bond after the curse had been lifted, the discovery of where to find the Maw, and when it would awaken, the justice I had planned to serve, it was for nothing. It was over.

I had lost.

My only hope was that the Maw had devoured Arystic the Shade while I had slept.

I began down the mountain. Alone.

Forgiveness

31

Have you ever sat alone on the eve of an important day, with nothing but your thoughts? Life jaunts on as you sit there as stone, and an unparalleled calmness washes over you. Perhaps you sit in meditation, or, like me, on a soft cushioned armchair with lilts of music that fill the air and dance at the edges of your thoughts. The worries of tomorrow's vital, unavoidable tasks somehow slip your conscious, and you are given the purest moment of bliss one can experience. There is, truly, no greater peace.

Elijah? a familiar voice asked. I opened my eyes to see him standing in front of me, the evening light casting its long shadows, inviting him in. He was old. Tired. I had never noticed it before, though now it was unmistakable. A recognition only to be gained when one becomes old and tired themselves, it would seem.

"Hello, Shadow," I said. My smile was unavoidable at seeing my long-lost friend. I had been so worried he would not make it. "It's been a while."

Too long, he said, and a smile of his own touched his voice.

"You're cutting it close, you know."

I was not entirely sure you would want to see me again. After the mountain.

My memory flashed to the scene. The open-mouthed Maw awaiting its sacrifice. Shadow and me, fighting. The hate. The searing hot pain that still scarred our shoulders. Oh, how I've regretted my actions that day.

"Please, forgive me. I was young and angry and new to freedom."

There is nothing I have not already forgiven.

My smile returned. I had missed him. I remember how much I despised him, wanted him out of my life, but I hadn't considered just how lonely my life would be without him. I thought marriage would replace him, or children, and while I loved them all with my whole heart, it wasn't the same. They were wonderful peripheries, but peripheries all the same. Shadow was a piece of me, a part of my soul. He could not be replaced. Only missed.

"You're sure this is what you want?" I asked. "There's no guarantee it will work."

Soltr did not return after... what happened. He spoke carefully, which I appreciated.

"You must admit this circumstance is different."

True, but I would rather risk being Bound for another one hundred lifetimes for the chance at a peaceful death. His surety was reassuring.

"In that case," I said, "you have an enthusiastic invitation to join me tonight."

With that, I felt Shadow's familiar coil wrap around me, linking my soul to his. The hole at my core flooded with his cool embrace. We were Bound. Once a strange definition, but now I understood there was nothing else that could describe our link. Our Bind.

I closed my eyes and leaned my head back. All was right. My family was taken care of, my soul was complete, and my music was wonderful. The importance of tomorrow could come at this very moment, and I would be content. I did not fear my responsibility. Whatever lay beyond would be welcoming to me and Shadow. And, with any luck, Victoria would be there. I sat in unparalleled comfort, waiting for my important day.

Waiting for my death.

About the Author

Quain Holtey is a writer and game designer with a BFA in creative writing and an MS in game design, and he can talk to you forever about absolutely nothing if you let him. In his (very) spare time, he game masters for his tabletop RPG group, writes short stories, and dreams of traveling the world.

Made in the USA
Las Vegas, NV
17 January 2024

84235180R00125